Virtuous

Genesis Two Eighteen Series

Jayme Moore Llewellyn

Copyright © 2014, 2017 Jayme Moore Llewellyn

All rights reserved.

ISBN:1545208751
ISBN-13:9781545208755

DEDICATION

This book is lovingly dedicated to my husband and best friend, Randy. You are the finest man I have ever known, and I am truly honored to be your wife. You have been a wonderful example of Ephesians 5:25: "Husbands, love your wives, even as Christ also loved the church, and gave himself for it."

Copyright © 2014, 2017 by Jayme Moore Llewellyn All rights reserved.

All rights reserved. No part of this publication may be reproduced, distributed, or transmitted in any form or by any means, including photocopying, recording, or other electronic or mechanical methods, without the prior written permission of the publisher, except in the case of brief quotations embodied in critical reviews and certain other noncommercial uses permitted by copyright law.
All scripture is taken from the King James Bible.
This novel is a work of fiction. Names, descriptions, entities, and incidents included in the story are products of the author's imagination. Any resemblance to actual persons, events, and entities is entirely coincidental.

Printed in the United States of America
Second Edition

ACKNOWLEDGMENTS

I acknowledge and give honor and glory to my Heavenly Father, who has guided my thoughts and pen throughout this book.

Trust in the Lord with all thine heart; and lean not unto thine own understanding. In all thy ways acknowledge Him and He shall direct thy paths.

Special thanks to:

Jonathan and Sabrina Dixon, owners of Cake and All Things Yummy.

Anna Grace Senter (pictured, front cover)

Chapter One

"Breathe...relax...breathe." Sarah squeezed Bianca's hand and gently stroked her hair as she watched her father coach another baby into the world. She swabbed Bianca's face with a cool, wet cloth to keep her calm and comfortable.

Dr. Phillips patted her foot. "You're doing great. I think this next one may be it. Just hang in there."

This was nothing new for Bianca. It was her sixth child. But conditions were very poor in the northern plains of Honduras and medical equipment and supplies minimal. Dr. Mike Phillips had felt compelled to come to this country as a medical missionary when Sarah was only eleven years old. As the oldest of five siblings, the title of "nurse" was bestowed on her at a very early age. She had followed her father through every muddy path and over every mountain within twenty miles. Her childhood home in Texas was a distant memory, as she would be twenty-eight on her birthday next month.

"Okay, Mrs. Ortega. This is it! Breathe…now push! Come on! Thaaaat's it." Sarah watched her father begin to smile as she saw the tiny form drop into the towel. She stepped over and took the baby to clear the air passages and clean the delicate skin with a soft, clean towel. Heartbeat? Good. Breathing? Good. Ten little fingers and ten little toes? All accounted for.

Dr. Phillips smiled down at Bianca. "Well, Mrs. Ortega. Looks like you've got another boy!"

He stooped to brush a kiss across her fingers, and Bianca gave him a weak smile. "Gracias, Doctor."

Sarah had always been amazed at her father's ability to bond with his patients. They had a trust in him that had come from years of experience and hard-earned respect. Born and bred in Texas, he looked the part, always wearing his cowboy hat that shaded his ever-present, broad smile. He was known throughout the village as an honorable man, and that meant more to Sarah than anything.

The baby decided to exercise his lungs and let out a loud squawk. Sarah lowered him down into Bianca's arms. "What will you call him?"

She gently took her new son and cradled him close. "We decided if it was a boy, he would be called Antonio."

"That's a beautiful name." Sarah smiled and ran a finger down his soft cheek. "Welcome to the world, Antonio. This is your birthday."

Mike swung open the door and called out, "Jose! Come and meet your new son!"

Jose came through the door practically running and knelt at the bedside. This was always Sarah's favorite part of delivering a baby…watching the reaction of the father. She had seen the most rugged, rough, and tough men reduce to silly-faced, baby-babbling softies when holding their son or daughter for the first time. After five sons already, she thought Jose would have lost a bit of his excitement, but she was just as pleased to watch him this time, as she had been with all the others before. He carefully took Antonio from Bianca and bounced him easily in his arms. He looked at Dr. Phillips with a broad smile. "He looks like his beautiful mother!"

As he cradled his son close, he leaned over to kiss Bianca on the forehead. "God has given us another tiny miracle."

Dr. Phillips quietly stepped over to kneel at the bedside. "Let us pray.

"Our gracious heavenly Father, we humbly bow to thank you for your mercy and grace upon this family. We pray for your guiding hand to lead them in the training and nurture of baby Antonio. May this home forever be centered in you. In Jesus's name, amen."

Mike Phillips stood and plopped his big cowboy hat on his head.

He patted Jose on the shoulder. "Jose, you take good care of these two. I'll send Rebekah over tomorrow to help out."

Sarah's sister, Rebekah, had helped many ladies during the days following childbirth. Mike was very proud of his two daughters and the fine ladies they had become. He credited that to God and their mother. Katherine had trained them well.

"Ah! Gracias, Doctor." Jose took his hand and shook it excitedly all the way to the door. "Gracias! Gracias, Doctor! Gracias!"

When they stepped out onto the porch, the air was thick with humidity…typical of the Honduran climate. This region was called the Mosquito Coast and known for its two seasons…hot and hotter. Dr. Phillips leaned against one of the support posts holding up the tiny front porch and looked at his watch while taking out a handkerchief from his back pocket to swab his face. He blew out a long sigh and looked at the time. "Whew. Four thirty." It had been a long night. The sun would be rising soon, and Sarah could see the tired lines in her father's face.

It occurred to her for the first time that he was not as young and vibrant as he used to be. The life of a missionary was not only nonstop and full of triumphs, but also full of cares. Being the only doctor in the area, they had seen everything from a happy childbirth, like what they had just experienced, to malaria and emergency amputations. Life was certainly a roller-coaster ride of emotion that required a great deal of self-control, even when things seemed out of control. And her father was constantly reminding her that ultimately, it was God who was in control.

He blew out a long sigh. "Well, let's go, Sarah."

He stepped off the porch, pulling his medical bag onto his shoulder, and they began their two-mile walk back home. They strolled in silence down the path that led back to their little, modest home, feeling the tiredness in their bones. Sarah felt that if she went to sleep, she could walk this familiar path with her eyes closed. Then her father spoke, pulling her out of the sleepy fog.

"Sarah, I appreciate your help tonight."

She glanced over at him with a tired smile. "You're welcome, Dad. I'm always amazed every time a new life is brought into the world. I think childbirth is the only *happy* occasion that a doctor is called for."

"You know, you're not a nurse anymore. You're just as much a doctor as I am." He stopped and turned to look at her with concerned eyes. "I want to talk to you about something, and I don't quite know how to say it."

Sarah had learned everything she knew from her father. She had been with him for so long that she knew what he was thinking before he thought it. But tonight...tonight was different. She had noticed his quiet demeanor over the last few weeks. His silence was deafening. It was the first time in a long time that she had not been able to figure out what was bothering him.

"Sarah, I am so proud of you for finishing medical school. But I'm just as proud of you for many other things. You have a loving heart, compassion toward others, and a great knowledge in the medical field. God has given you wisdom to know how to use that knowledge. Over the years, I've come to depend on you more than I realized." He looked down as he pulled his bag up farther on his shoulder, and she could see his eyes fighting back the tears. He finally looked back at her.

"You've been a joy to your mother and me. I remember when you gave your life to Christ at such an early age, and I prayed that God would use you in a wonderful way. You've been a light to everyone you've touched, and I know you came back to help me with my mission. But that's just it. It's *my* mission. It's what God called *me* to do. If I could allow myself to be selfish and keep you here, I would. But God gave you to me, so that I could train you to go and fulfill what God has for *your* life. I know it's always been your dream to go back to America, and I also know about the letter from Bro. John Hawks in Colorado. I want you to know that your mother and I have been praying that God would give you guidance.

But knowing you as I do, you won't go unless you're sure that all is well here. So, Sarah, I'm letting you know. All is well."

She had been focused on her father for so long—learning his skills, adopting his mannerisms—that she hadn't noticed how well he also knew her. She had been praying about this for a long time, after receiving the letter from Bro. Hawks and his wife, ministering to orphans in the Denver area. She loved children and would welcome an opportunity to help. Hard work would be the prescription for such a venture, and she was certainly no stranger to that. But feeling a loyalty to her family, she had not dared to think on it too much…until now.

She stepped close and stretching up on tiptoes, wrapped her arms around his neck. "Thank you, Dad. I love you, so much. It excites me to think about going back to the States and scares me at the same time. I've always had my family around me for strength."

"Honey, I know we'll miss you terribly. But it's time for you to spread your wings and let God be your strength." He placed a kiss on top of her head. "I just want you to know that I trust you completely. Whatever you decide, your mother and I will support you wholeheartedly."

"I know, Dad, and you don't know how much that means to me. I want to do the right thing. Just keep praying."

He smiled down at her. "I'll do that. Now, let's get home before your mother sends out a search party." They chuckled, and Sarah wrapped her arm in his as they walked among the palms and evergreens toward home.

The ER doctor stepped into the waiting room, his hands tucked into his lab coat pockets. There were several families milling around and talking softly, waiting for news of a loved one. He looked around until he spotted Mrs. Patrick waiting over next to the coffee machine. As he got closer, he could see the anxiety of the unknown that filled her face. Her daughter, Elizabeth, had leaned close to drape a concerned arm around her shoulders.

"Mrs. Patrick?" Mary Patrick looked up at him with tired eyes. She slowly stood, waiting the prognosis.

"Mrs. Patrick, it seems that your husband has had a stroke, called a cerebral thrombosis. That's when a clot forms in a major artery to the brain. It's often caused by high blood pressure." He crossed his arms and in a very matter-of-fact, loud, and insensitive manner, said, "I've seen better, and I've seen worse. He'll definitely need some therapy, and I'll prescribe some medication to help with his high blood pressure problem. He has slurred speech and paralysis on his right side. I really don't expect him to fully recover."

Elizabeth reached over to steady her mother as she received the dreaded news and began to sway under the stress. Mary finally turned into her daughter's shoulder to cry softly, and Elizabeth eased her back down into the chair. She resented the cool demeanor of Dr. Garmon and decided that she didn't care for his candor concerning her father. The truth could sometimes be harsh, but a little compassion would certainly help, and this doctor could use a good dose of it. He had no feeling. No compassion. Nothing. It was clear that her father was just another number on his list of patients for the day.

Elizabeth lowered her voice, trying to avoid upsetting her mother any further. "Dr. Garmon, isn't there any hope of him recovering from this?"

Dr. Garmon smirked. "I wouldn't count on it."

This was intolerable behavior. Was he this cold and calloused with all his patients? Elizabeth felt her face get hot. "Well, we'll see about that."

She gently pulled her mother from the chair, whirled her around, and started down the hall. She could hear him call after her. "He's in room 203."

The indignation with Dr. Garmon had caused her steps to be quick and determined, but as she approached the room, his words began to sink into her heart, and suddenly her feet felt very heavy. Slurred speech. Paralysis. Her hand trembled as she reached out to push the door open. The man that had hit a few tennis balls with her yesterday would be far different today.

The room was still and quiet, except for the steady beep of monitors. The bathroom light was the only illumination to see the crumpled form in the slightly-raised, adjustable bed. Elizabeth steadied her mother as they stepped around the bed to look at his face. He was awake and tried to smile, but the right side of his face was badly pulled to one side. Elizabeth watched her mother steady herself with determination and bend down to kiss his cheek.

"Jack? Can you hear me?" He tried to say something, but the words simply wouldn't form.

She patted his hand. "It's all right, sweetheart. You don't have to say anything. Honey, the doctor says you've had a stroke. You may have a little trouble with your speech and your right side, but I believe that God will give you a full recovery from this. We'll do our part and depend on God to do the rest."

Elizabeth knew that her mother was trying to be positive for her father's sake. She looked away as a tear rolled down his cheek. But Mary had found strength beyond understanding. She pulled up a chair to his bedside and leaned toward him so that her face was just inches from his.

"Jack, we've been through a lot together, and by the grace of God, we'll get through this too."

She brushed away his tear with the back of her hand. "I love you, Jack. I won't leave you. Get some rest now, and when you wake up, I'll be here."

With his left hand, he touched his own lips and then touched hers.

Their quiet moment was interrupted by a bold knock on the door that was followed by Dr. Garmon making his boisterous entrance into the room. Elizabeth thought it would have been nice if he could have given them just a few moments of privacy, but given his previous behavior, that would have been too out of character.

"Well, it looks like you'll be going home tomorrow, Mr. Patrick."

Elizabeth looked sharply. "So soon?!"

"Yes. There's no reason to keep him here any longer. We've done all we can do. The nurse will help you schedule a ???follow-up appointment with my office before you leave the hospital. He'll also need physical and speech therapy on a weekly basis. We'll talk about that when you come to my office. Well, good luck, Mr. Patrick." And he breezed back out the door as quickly as he had breezed in.

Mary sat still for a moment and then slapped her knee and stood smartly. "Elizabeth, we need to pray that God will give us the right doctor. I don't believe this Dr. Garmon is what we need."

Elizabeth watched her mother begin tucking the covers and adjusting the bed. Then she paged the nurse to come and refresh his cup of water. Now this was the mom she knew…confident, together, and equal to the task. But she also knew that this was how her mother dealt with heartache. She stayed busy…very busy.

Elizabeth walked up behind Mary as she began dusting the window seal with a damp paper towel and wrapped her arms around her mother's neck, stopping her for just a moment, holding on tight. "Mom, please let me call Dave. He would want to know."

Mary sighed and patted her daughter's arm. "I know, Elizabeth. I just didn't want to call him until we knew exactly what had happened. He's going to be upset, but he's half a world away. There's nothing he can do from New York. Just break it to him as easy as you can. Tell him we plan to be back home tomorrow, so there's no rush to fly back tonight. He can wait till in the morning. Tell him that we need his prayers more than anything right now."

Elizabeth's pumps clacked down the tile hallway to the family waiting area. She was glad that her parents and Dave believed in a God. It really wasn't her thing, but if it helped them, she could deal with it for now.

Most of the families who had been waiting throughout the evening were gone, with the exception of a couple who sat on the far side of the room watching the flat-screen television. Elizabeth made her way to the far corner for some privacy and sank down into the cloth-covered chair. She was the youngest of the family and very protective of her brother. She knew it was ridiculous to think of herself as his protector. He was six-foot-three inches of pure muscle, and she was five-foot-four…if you count her two-inch heels. Dave lived a very luxurious life, but one that placed him under an enormous amount of pressure. Being in the public eye had its advantages, but as far as she could see, the disadvantages were far greater.

Her fingers trembled as she dialed the numbers. Oh, how she dreaded this conversation. Her mind grasped for words as she held the phone to her ear and listened to it ring on the other end. *I don't know what to say. Dave and Dad are so close. I know this is going to be a terrible shock to him.*

When he answered, she could tell he was out of breath.

"Hi, sis! What's up?"

"Uh...hello, Dave. Did I catch you in the middle of a workout?"

"I'm always in the middle of something. But I'm never too busy for my favorite gal. How's everything on the home front?"

With heartbeat racing, she swallowed hard as she tried to control her trembling voice.

"That's...why I'm calling." She let out a long sigh and closed her eyes. She rubbed her forehead, trying to erase the throbbing. "We're at the hospital. Dad's not well."

"Why? What happened?" She could hear the concern in his voice and sought for a way to ease the blow, but there was just no way to soften the words as they slowly rolled from her lips.

"Dad...had a stroke."

Silence. More silence.

"Dave, are you there?"

He slowly responded with a low and steady voice as he absorbed her words. "I'm here. How bad was it? How's Mom?"

"He has some paralysis and slurred speech. Mom was pretty shaken at first, but you know Mom. She's strong...and trying to stay busy. If I don't stop her, she'll be cleaning the entire second floor." Elizabeth was trying to keep the conversation as light as possible, which was hard to do in the face of the terrible reality. But there was nothing David could do from the other side of the country.

"Tell Mom I'll catch the first plane home tonight."

"The doctor says Dad can go home tomorrow, so Mom wanted me to tell you to get a good night's rest and wait until tomorrow to fly back. She also wanted me to ask you to pray."

"Pray, I can do, but a good night's rest?" She could hear his frustrated tone. "I'll be home tonight. See you soon, Liz."

His decision was firm, and she knew better than to protest. "Be careful, Dave."

Elizabeth clicked off her cell phone and stared at the floor, trying to think of what to do next. This all seemed like a terrible nightmare, and it was so hard to gather her thoughts. She bowed her head into her hands, wishing she could erase this day. It had started so well this morning when she joined her parents at the breakfast table. But when her father collapsed, falling out of his chair and into the kitchen floor, life changed in a hurry. The day had been nothing more than a flurry of flashing lights, doctors, nurses, and general chaos.

When she returned to her father's room, her mother was sitting in the little chair beside the bed where she could hold his hand. At first glance, Elizabeth thought she was praying, but as she tiptoed inside and drew closer, she realized that her mother was sound asleep. The exhaustion of the day had finally taken its toll. Mary's face was streaked with dried tears. Elizabeth stooped to kiss her cheek and lay a blanket across her shoulders. Then she eased herself down into the nearby recliner. She leaned her head back into the chair and closed her eyes, hoping that when morning came, it would all have been a bad dream. Something stirred deep within her soul that cried out for peace. And for the first time in her life, she wished that she could pray too.

Chapter Two

Early Thursday morning, Sarah Phillips was on her way to the office, meditating on all the things God had provided since she had been in the States. Being in a practice with another doctor had made things so much easier in many ways. The fact that Dr. Barlow was a Christian was such a blessing. God had used John and Jennifer Hawks to recommend her to Tom Barlow, who had taken her under his wing ever since she had arrived. She loved watching the doctor and his wife, Carol. They had just celebrated their fortieth wedding anniversary, and their spark was definitely still shining bright. They genuinely enjoyed one another's company and reminded her of her own parents in the way they secretly flirted with one another. Whenever Carol Barlow came to the office, her husband would stop whatever he was doing to give her a big bear hug. It was a relationship that spread sunshine. Today was Thursday, which meant that Mrs. Carol would probably show up after lunch with a big batch of her homemade chocolate chip cookies. And by the looks of Dr. Barlow, he had eaten plenty of them. Sarah smiled when she thought of him patting his big round belly and saying, "Well, I would go on a diet, but I've got too much invested." Maybe it was just the excitement of a new job, but Sarah had a feeling she was really going to enjoy working here.

She pulled into her parking place behind the building and headed toward the back door that was close to her personal office. Sliding into her lab coat, she walked toward the receptionist's window to check the patient list for the day. Mmmmm...coffee. She could always count on Millie for a good cup of coffee in the morning. Millie was on the phone when she entered the office area so she began pouring her cup quietly. Whoever she was talking to, she seemed extremely nervous, which was very unusual. Millie Tompkins was a people person who was always bubbly and cheerful with plenty to say. But she wasn't saying much at the moment, which concerned Sarah. This mystery caller had rendered the talkative receptionist speechless. Sarah stood by the coffee counter and watched as Millie slowly put down the receiver.

"Is everything okay, Millie?"

She quickly turned to Sarah. "Dr. Phillips! I didn't know you had come in. That call was for you."

Sarah was still trying to figure out what had Millie so shaken. She casually stood, leaning against the counter, stirring the cream in her coffee. "That's all right. I can always call them back." She tapped the stirring spoon on the side of her mug and set it on a napkin. "Who was it? Did they leave a message?"

"You're never going to believe this, but that was Mary Patrick. She said that a missionary friend of hers had recommended you and suggested she call. She would like to meet with you this afternoon. I looked at your schedule and told her you could come around four o'clock. Is that all right?"

The name Mary Patrick didn't mean a thing to her, but judging by Millie's reaction, this Ms. Patrick must be well-to-do. Sarah didn't want to seem naive by telling Millie that she didn't have a clue who she was talking about. She already felt plenty awkward trying to adjust to her new American life. The missionary friends to whom Millie had referred must have been John and Jennifer. Funny, she had just talked to Jennifer an hour ago, and the name Mary Patrick wasn't mentioned.

"Yes. Four o'clock will be fine. Do I need to call Ms. Patrick and confirm the time?"

"No. I told her if anything changed I would call her back. Otherwise, she could expect you at four."

Sarah started down the hallway toward her office when she turned to look back. "Millie? Do you have directions to the Patrick home?"

The receptionist swung around in her chair. "Do you mean you've lived here three months and you haven't noticed the entrance to the Patrick Estate?"

Suddenly, Sarah remembered passing huge brick columns and a black iron gate with a golden "P" in the center of it out on Milton Road. The house wasn't visible from the main highway, but the winding road, just past the beautifully landscaped entrance, was lazy and long, lined with lovely evergreen trees and shrubs.

"Oh! Yes, I do remember. It's on Milton Road, isn't it?"

She turned again to head toward her office. "If I'm going to make it by four, I had better get cracking."

Millie's voice trailed after her. "Boy, for someone who just got an invitation to the Patrick Estate, you sure are cool about it."

Sarah left the office around three o'clock, hoping to make it to her appointment in plenty of time. Although it had been a very busy day, the thought of Mrs. Patrick stayed tucked in the back of her mind. Millie had been giddy all day, one time poking her head in Sarah's office to ask, "Think you could get me an autograph?" Obviously, this was a well-known family, but for someone who had spent the better part of life outside the United States, wealth and prominence were of the unknown…especially wealth. Sarah could count on one hand the times that her father had received money. Most payment had come in the form of goods or services. She had to smile when she remembered the look on her mother's face when her father brought home pig's feet as a thank-you for helping a young man with his ingrown toe nail. She held up the jar of pink feet and teased, "Well, I guess the payment fits the treatment." Even though they didn't have much by way of material goods, she never remembered hearing her mother complain of not having enough. Oh, how she missed her family! She loved them all, but lately she had especially missed Rebekah, who was the youngest of the family. Whenever she needed someone to confide in, Rebekah was an understanding ear.

Sarah was pulled from her thoughts of home as she turned onto Milton Road. Elegant houses lined the road on both sides until it turned to all woodland. After about a mile of lovely green forest, the Patrick Estate entrance rose in the distance.

Sarah pulled up to the gate, pushed the button on the intercom, and gave her name. She could feel the thump of her heart quicken as the enormous gate began to ease open. The winding drive was nearly a half-mile long. Whoever the Patrick's were, they certainly wanted their privacy. The wooded drive finally curved into a clearing, revealing an amazing three-story brick home with sparkling glass windows stretching from the top floor to the bottom. It extended in every direction with various rooflines. To the right was a four-car garage that would dwarf most any house she had ever seen. Millie had not mentioned to Sarah why Mrs. Patrick wished to see her. She let out a long sigh, gathered her nervous jitters, and stepped out of the car to climb the numerous steps leading to the large, wooden front door. After ringing the doorbell, she could hear quick footsteps drawing closer and the clicking of the lock. A thick Spanish accent greeted her.

"May I help you?"

Well, this wasn't exactly a cure for her homesickness, but seeing those sparkling black eyes and lovely brown skin reminded her of the many friends she had left behind. This lady had a keen resemblance to her dear friend Bianca. It seemed like forever since she had been able to use her Spanish.

"Hola! Mi nombre es Dr. Phillips. Senora Patrick es esperar me."

With the address in Spanish, the little lady's face lit up like a Christmas tree. They exchanged a few pleasantries, and Sarah learned that her name was Maria. Already, there was a warm friendliness between them that helped settle Sarah's nerves. Maria led her down the hallway to the left and into what was obviously the library. Bookshelves extending from floor to ceiling lined every wall except for the far side of the room, which boasted an elegant and cozy rock fireplace. The plush furnishings and rich burgundy area rug that stretched over the dark wooden floor made the room very warm and inviting. Too nervous to sit, Sarah meandered over to look at some of the books. There was also a great deal of baseball memorabilia. Framed newspaper clippings of baseball games, photos of players, as well as what looked to be a whole row of plaques and awards, lined both sides of the fireplace. Obviously, the man of the house was a big baseball fan. She started across the room to take a closer look but stopped short as she heard the knob on the large, wooden door turn. Two ladies entered the room. The first was Mrs. Mary Patrick, a small, petite lady of about sixty years. Her white hair was tucked into a very stylish arrangement, and her eyes were kind and friendly. She extended a hand to Sarah and began the introductions.

"Hello, I'm Mary Patrick, and this is my daughter Elizabeth."

Elizabeth was of the same build as her mother. Lovely red curls fell around her shoulders indicative of her Irish ancestry, and her brown eyes reflected the same warmth. Sarah felt a spirit of kinship that put her completely at ease as she took the elder lady's hand into her own.

"I'm Dr. Sarah Phillips, and I'm pleased to meet you both."

The two ladies sat on the plush Queen Ann sofa, while Sarah took her place in the leather winged-back chair. The room was very welcoming with its soft lighting and the smell of antiquity from all of the surrounding hardwood and books.

"Dr. Phillips, I want to thank you for coming today. I'm sure you're wondering why I've called you here."

"Yes, ma'am. The receptionist didn't mention the reason for your call."

Mary Patrick folded her hands in her lap and heaved a sigh. "Well, you see, my husband, Jack, recently had a stroke."

"Oh, I see. I'm sorry to hear that, Mrs. Patrick."

"Yes. It happened about three weeks ago. We were sitting together at breakfast when he suddenly collapsed. It was quite a shock as you can imagine. The hospital staff was wonderful, and we were very pleased with his treatment while he was there. However, we were not satisfied with the attending physician and felt that we should look elsewhere for Jack's continuing care. I had mentioned this to Jennifer Hawks, and she immediately suggested that I call you. We already have a speech and physical therapist, but I would like to talk with you about serving as Jack's prime physician. I have a great deal of confidence in Bro. Hawks and his wife Jennifer, but I would like to know a little bit about you and your background, if I may."

"Yes, ma'am, of course. I assisted my father, a missionary doctor in Honduras, for seventeen years.

Mrs. Patrick wrinkled her brow. "Seventeen years? You can't be more than twenty-five."

Sarah chuckled. "Actually, I'm twenty-eight, but I began assisting my father at the age of eleven." Mary and Elizabeth sat in stunned silence as Sarah continued.

"God allowed me to minister in four Central American countries when I was a teenager, and I attended the University of San Pedro Sula to complete my medical degree six months ago. I'm currently working at Mountain Family Medicine with Dr. Tom Barlow." Sarah leaned forward in her chair. "All of that is very important. But the most important thing you need to know about me, Mrs. Patrick, is the fact that I'm a Christian. I asked Jesus to be my savior and to guide my life when I was eight years old. I've seen his faithfulness time and time again, and I believe that God allowed this into the life of your family for a purpose far greater than what we can now understand. Every single life is precious in the sight of God. If you entrust me with the care of your husband, I will not only care for his physical needs, but I will make his health a matter of prayer each day, as I do all of my patients."

Elizabeth put an arm around her mother. "I understand that you have an office, but it would be so much better if you could come here...perhaps in the evenings. I believe it would make things easier for Mom. Of course, we would be willing to pay you for this service."

Sarah looked thoughtful for a moment. "My time in Honduras consisted solely of house calls since there wasn't a local hospital to service the area where we lived. My father and I made rounds to our patients every day. Ms. Patrick, I'm honored that you would consider me to care for your father, and I'm happy to offer whatever services I can to make this easier. But given my workload, I would only be able to come once a week. Would that be acceptable?"

Elizabeth glanced at her mother, who gave her a slight nod. "Yes. I think that would work for us."

Sarah took out a pen and pad. "Mrs. Patrick, can you tell me what your husband did for a living before the stroke?"

"He owned a construction company for twenty-nine years. He retired three years ago when we decided to move to Denver."

"I see. And how old is Mr. Patrick?"

Mrs. Patrick gave a sly grin. "He's sixty-four and very handsome. May I introduce him to you?"

Sarah smiled as she tucked her pen and pad back into her bag. "Absolutely!"

Mrs. Patrick looked at her daughter. "Well, Elizabeth. Let's go introduce Dr. Phillips to your father."

Sarah followed them back down the hallway and up the long staircase to the second floor. Elizabeth slowed her steps to fall back with Sarah. "Have you enjoyed your time in Colorado so far?"

Sarah smiled. "Yes, I'm enjoying it a great deal. Unfortunately, I've been so busy that I haven't had much time for sightseeing. But it is a lovely place."

"Do you play tennis?"

Sarah looked at her with an apologetic glance. "I've…never played tennis. I'm afraid I wouldn't know what to do."

"What if I teach you?" Elizabeth said it so energetically that Sarah hated to refuse.

She shrugged a shoulder. "I…guess…I could try."

"Great! What about tomorrow? The weather has been unseasonably warm for November, and the weather forecast looks great for the next few days. What do you say?"

"I get off at four o'clock. Would four thirty be too late?"

"No. Not at all. I'll look forward to it!"

By the time they had reached the second floor, Sarah found herself looking forward to getting to know Elizabeth. She reminded her so much of her sister, Rebekah, with her welcoming smiles and ease of conversation.

At first, Sarah wondered why Mr. Patrick was on the second floor since that would seem a bit inconvenient given his condition, but when she entered the large bedroom, she understood his choice completely. Cream-colored walls, an almond shade of rug over the hardwood floor, and forest green bedding, accented with touches of gold, gave the room an open and airy feel. A huge bay window with a panoramic view of the rising snow-capped Rocky Mountains in the distance gave the feeling of being outdoors…even if that were not possible. And judging from the man tucked under the covers of the big, king-sized bed, physical activity was out of the realm of possibility for the time being.

Elizabeth reached over to gently shake her father's shoulder. "Dad? The doctor's here."

He slightly opened one eye, and Mary carefully raised his back while Elizabeth adjusted the pillows for him to sit up.

Sarah could tell that it had been a rather moderate stroke, and her heart immediately went out to this man. His face, a sun-kissed brown, revealed his love of the outdoors. His soft, brown eyes, reflected kindness like that of Mary and Elizabeth. Flecks of gray peppered his once-dark hair, and he tried to ease a crooked smile on his lips. She took hold of his large, limp hand and presented her warmest expression.

"Hello, Mr. Patrick. My name is Sarah Phillips."

Mary came up beside Sarah and laid a hand on his arm.

"Sweetheart, this is the doctor that I was telling you about. The one Bro. John Hawks recommended."

Elizabeth drew up a chair for Sarah next to the bedside. She made herself comfortable as she began to tell her life story all over again to Mr. Patrick. He never said a word, but there was an unspoken calm in the room…a feeling of the Lord's peace. Although the stroke had taken its toll, Jack Patrick was not a frail man by any measure. Judging by his broad shoulders, he had been very active and strong before the stroke, and Sarah wanted more than anything to help him regain his independence again. She could see the feeling of helplessness in his eyes. Oh! How she wanted to give him hope of a full recovery!

"Mr. Patrick, I want you to know that if I can be of service to you and your family, I will do my best to serve your needs. I know that you will be praying about this decision and so will I." With a smile, she squeezed his hand. "You get some rest now."

She stood and turned to Mary. "Mrs. Patrick, here's my card. We'll take this to the Lord in prayer, and if you have peace about me being your physician, I would be honored." And Sarah walked out of the room to wait in the hallway.

Mary was a bit astonished at Sarah's easy demeanor. Most doctors would have jumped at the chance to be private physician for her family, given their financial status. Apparently, that didn't mean a thing to this lovely, young missionary doctor, which automatically put her up a few notches in Mary's eyes. Every accolade that John and Jennifer had laid at Sarah's feet was beyond true.

After they descended the long staircase and said their good-byes, Mary and Elizabeth watched Dr. Phillips take her leave.

"Oh! Elizabeth. This is the most relief I've felt in three weeks. I know that young woman was a God-send. Did I hear you planning an outing tomorrow?"

"Yes. I invited her over for tennis." Elizabeth narrowed her eyes, looking thoughtful. "I really like her. She seems genuine."

Mary began the climb back up the stairs, talking as she went. "I think she is. John and Jennifer spoke very highly of her family. She seems to have a compassionate heart, and I don't think money is very high on her list of priorities, but modesty certainly is."

Elizabeth looked up at her mother, who had reached the top step. "What do you mean?"

She failed to mention that she graduated at the top of her class, she's bilingual, and even though she's a doctor, her main purpose in coming back to America was to help with the children's home. Jennifer said that she comes every evening to do odd jobs and help with the kids. She also serves as prime physician for all the children, and Jennifer said that she doesn't charge a dime."

Elizabeth walked over to one of the large windows and stood with arms crossed to watch Sarah climb in her modest, compact car. Elizabeth had enjoyed very few friends in her lifetime. Her childhood was happy enough, but Dave's fame and fortune had brought such a sense of caution that she dared not get close to anyone. Her brother meant the world to her, and even though she wasn't into religion herself, she was very proud of him. He had reached out to help many hurting people, and she meant to protect him from the snares of those who sought to destroy his good name.

There had been times that she had let her guard down and accepted what she thought was an honest friendship…only to find out that her *friend* was just using her to get close to her handsome, eligible brother. It was obvious that Sarah Phillips claimed to be a Christian, but didn't they all? The hypocrisy that she had seen among people claiming to know God was sickening. It seemed that people just wanted to seem religious for personal gain, like money or some kind of reputation. Elizabeth stared out the window, watching the car taillights disappear down the drive. Well, time would tell if this Dr. Phillips was the real deal. But as first impressions go, she had to admit, she was impressed.

Chapter Three

Sarah followed Elizabeth out to the stone patio that overlooked the lovely, manicured back lawn with the majestic Rocky Mountains in the distance. They strolled down the little path, paved with stepping stones, leading to the tennis court. Sarah still wondered in the back of her mind what could have brought this family such an obvious amount of wealth. She had very little experience with the wealthy, but in her mind, people were just people. Her father used to say, "Everybody puts their boots on one at a time." She had to smile as she thought about their little house in Central America. Why, they were considered well-to-do when they got indoor plumbing. But the Patrick's had been so congenial that it was easy to get past any intimidation concerning their position in the world…whatever it was.

When they reached the court, Elizabeth began her instruction on the finer points of tennis. Forehand, backhand, volley, and finally, the serve…which Sarah found to be a bit tricky, but she eventually caught on.

After several rounds of volleys, they met beside the net to sit on the wooden bench and caught their breath. Elizabeth picked up a towel out of her duffel bag to wipe the sweat from her face and arms while Sarah took out a water bottle from her own bag.

"You catch on quick! Are you sure you've never played tennis before?"

Sarah raised her eyebrows and gave a wry grin. "Positive. To my recollection, I never even *saw* a tennis court in Honduras."

"So, what kind of games did you play?"

"Well, to be honest, there was very little time for play. My father and I hit the ground running before sunup and usually didn't return until late evening." She chuckled. "There was this one game we used to play called poison stick, but you wouldn't want to know about that. It involved a long stick and an outhouse." Her chuckle turned to full laughter as she thought about her childhood antics.

Elizabeth quirked an eyebrow and laughed. "You're right. I wouldn't want to know. So how many siblings do you have?"

"I'm the oldest. Then there's Tim, Luke, Micah, and my sister, Rebekah. Tim is Mr. Responsible. Luke is Mr. Protector. Micah is the explorer of the family, and Rebekah is just pure tender heart. We didn't have many toys and things when we were kids, but we had the great outdoors and big imaginations. I'm surprised my mom still has her sanity."

"It must have been nice growing up in a big family like that."

"Oh, I wouldn't trade my memories for the world. I miss all my family, but especially my sister. We're very close. I hope she can come and visit me once I get settled."

Elizabeth took a long drink of her orange sports drink. "I look forward to meeting her. Are you two very much alike?"

"Not really. But I guess that's why we get along so well. We complement each other in a lot of ways. I'm her motivator, and she's my encourager. I motivate her to cultivate her talents, and she encourages me to go beyond my limits and never quit. Rebekah is very gifted in many areas. She's always been soft-spoken and shy, but I believe those are her gifts too. Rebekah has a way with people, and they find her easy to talk to. She makes them feel relaxed and comfortable around her. I really miss her."

"Yeah, I know what you mean. I've always been close to my brother Dave even though he's not home very much these days."

"You never mentioned a brother. What does he do?"

Elizabeth paused to absorb the question, glanced at Sarah, and then leaned back laughing, losing her breath completely a couple of times. She was reveling in the humor until she realized that Sarah wasn't laughing with her. She caught her breath long enough to stop and look at Sarah who, to her amazement, had a totally bewildered and confused look on her face. Could it be that she honestly doesn't know who David Patrick is? This couldn't be possible. But the look on Sarah's face told her that it *was* possible.

"Are you serious? You really don't know who my brother is?" her eyes wide in astonishment.

Looking apologetic and somewhat embarrassed, Sarah shook her head and narrowed her eyes. "I'm sorry, Elizabeth, but I really don't." She lifted her eyebrows. "Should I?"

"Dave is the starting pitcher for the Denver Wolves."

Sarah wrinkled her brow as she tried to understand and cocked her head to one side.

"The Denver Wolves?"

If Elizabeth had been astonished before, she was absolutely floored now as she realized that Sarah didn't even know who the Wolves were. "You know. The professional baseball team here in Denver."

Then Sarah's eyes had a glimmer of understanding, but she still didn't seem all that impressed either.

"Oh! Yes. I do recall seeing billboards about the team now…and your brother pitches for them? That must be a fascinating job!" She smiled her sweetest smile, not realizing the implications of her discovery.

"Yes. I think he really enjoys it," Elizabeth replied amusedly, knowing that Sarah had no idea what she had stumbled upon.

Elizabeth wanted to laugh again, but she wasn't sure if it was because of Sarah's sweet innocence or the fact that she had finally found someone that seemed to enjoy being her friend because of who *she* was…not because of who her brother was. If she had any reservations before, she certainly didn't have any now. Sarah Phillips was the real deal.

Chapter Four

David Patrick boarded the private plane bound for Atlanta, thankful for the three weeks he had been able to spend with his family. Nothing had prepared him for seeing his dad for the first time after the stroke. His slurred speech had made communication very hard, and David felt embarrassed every time he had to lean closer to try and understand the muddled phrases. He could see the frustration in his father's eyes from not being able to transfer his thoughts into clear words. Would his dad ever fully recover from this? Only God could answer that question. He closed his eyes. *Dear God, if it be your will, please grant Dad a full recovery and make us all stronger from this.*

Elizabeth had called just minutes after he arrived at the airport to let him know that the interview with the new doctor had gone very well. The relief in her voice was a comfort in itself. The conversation with Elizabeth had been brief, as he was trying to get everything in order and find his boarding area, but he was glad everything had gone well for his mother's sake. He could see the exhaustion in her eyes and felt it in her slumped shoulders as he hugged her good-bye. There was a definite feeling of guilt in having to leave home again. It seemed that he was just as busy during the off-season with speaking engagements, as he was during the regular season. The celebrity life was exciting and fast-paced, but there was something inside that tugged his thoughts back to a simpler time, when he and Liz spent their afternoons climbing trees or playing cowboys and Indians in the back yard of their Tennessee home. Or coming home on Sunday after church to a big lunch with all of the family. Or just lying in bed at night with the windows raised to feel the fresh, cool breeze and listen to the symphony of crickets.

Ah, Elizabeth. He couldn't imagine a better sister. She had always looked after things for him while he was away. But Liz was not a believer. She was convinced that she could go to heaven on personal merit. He had talked to her time and time again, but she would always compare her life to those that claimed to be Christians. She said if they could go to heaven, then she could too. She was very cautious of people and found it hard to get close to anyone. It hadn't escaped his attention that she hardly ever went out or had any close friends at all. He was also aware that the last "friend" had been using Elizabeth to get to him. She had been very hurt by the whole incident but never talked about it. It was absolutely disgusting at the lengths that women would go to these days to snare a man. He remembered that Elizabeth had invited her so-called friend to a Bible study their mom was having, but all she wanted to study was him...and was very obvious about it. She made excuses to follow him everywhere he went, talking loudly and laughing that shrill laugh that would make fingernails on a chalkboard seem soothing. They had been praying that the Bible study would help Liz see the truth about Jesus Christ, and it hurt when the girl became such a distraction that no one could focus on anything. He didn't know when acting like a lady had gone out of style, but apparently, it went out a long time ago since the only women that he would classify as "a real lady" was over the age of fifty. Through friends, family, speaking engagements, letters, and even total strangers, he had been introduced to countless women. All with that gleam in their eye that screamed, "I'm on a treasure hunt." There was just something distasteful about it all. He had to wonder if they would be so eager to make his acquaintance if he were just an everyday guy working a nine-to-five job. "People who are genuine," as his grandfather used to say, "are as rare as hen's teeth."

Yes. Celebrity definitely had a price tag...not that he was unthankful for all that God had blessed him with. He had been given so many opportunities to share the gospel with thousands of people, and the financial gain had allowed him to bring his parents and sister out to Colorado with him to share his home. He had given thousands to missions at home and abroad. But there was something missing. God had been faithful. God was so good. He felt more blessed than he deserved. But something was still missing. He settled back into his seat, took his Bible out of the little carry-on duffle, and began reading in Genesis chapter two until his eyes met verse eighteen:

And the Lord God said, "It is not good that the man should be alone; I will make him a help meet for him."

The words burned into his heart like a branding iron, and the loneliness engulfed him. He flipped his Bible to the book of Proverbs 31:10: "Who can find a virtuous woman? For her price is far above rubies." He blew out a long sigh. The thought of finding that special someone absolutely shook him to the core. After the decision to accept Christ as Savior, this was the next biggest step in life. He had seen what a loving, God-centered marriage could bring, but he had also witnessed heartbreak and destruction of a broken marriage, too many times to count. He had counseled many a teammate with marital woes, which seemed ironic since he had never been married himself, but it did open the door for him to share his faith in Jesus Christ. Many of the marriages had been built solely on the physical. It's true that physical attraction is the initial draw, but it had to be built on so much more than that. The Bible that he held in his hand said that "God is love." Without a relationship with the Lord, was true love even possible? Love in its deepest form had to come from its creator.

God has many attributes. God is the very essence of love. God created man and woman. God is the author of all that is pure and right. He leaned his head back against the headrest and closed his eyes.

God, You know my heart. I would rather be single the rest of my life than to make a bad decision. I don't trust my own judgment concerning this matter. I've met too many people who are not what they say they are. I feel confused. I feel guilty coming before you with a request because you have already blessed me beyond measure. You have given me my dream of baseball, a wonderful family, and material blessings as well. But you know that my heart is heavy concerning this subject of a help meet. At this moment, I give you full control over this part of my life. I place it completely in your capable hands. In Jesus's name. Amen.

As his eyes fluttered open, the peace and knowledge of God's sovereignty washed over him, and his mind returned to home and family. His mother had mentioned they would be having an after-Thanksgiving dinner party Friday evening with a few intimate friends. Her definition of *a few* was anywhere from five to one hundred, but he didn't care. It would just be good to get back home.

He glanced over at Steve, who had slumped down in his seat, with his long legs stretched out in front of him and a cowboy hat covering his face. Steve Travis was a former Texas Ranger and long-time friend. David knew he could trust Steve with his life and had made the decision to hire him for security when the publicity had made personal safety too much to handle. Steve was a new believer, and they had shared many a conversation over the last four years. But matters of the heart were something that Steve seemed indifferent to. In all the time that David had known him, he never knew Steve to date or show interest in anyone. His reason for leaving the Rangers was unknown, and David had never probed his friend for answers. He valued their friendship too much to step into territory that was clearly off-limits. Steve had spoken to him recently about returning to the Rangers someday, but it was not in the immediate future. He was a good man and would be hard to replace, but David closed his eyes again and settled back into his seat. He would worry about that when the time came. There was no use borrowing trouble.

Chapter Five

Driving back up the winding road leading to the Patrick Estate, Sarah didn't know what made her the happiest...the opportunity to help Mr. Patrick and his loving family, the sweet kids at the children's home, or the friendship with Elizabeth. The last few days had been wonderful and made the heaviness of homesickness seem much lighter. It was so nice of Mrs. Patrick to invite her to dinner. Celebrating Thanksgiving alone had been tolerable knowing that she would be coming to the Patrick home this evening. Bro. John Hawks and Jennifer were planning to attend as well. Words couldn't express how privileged she felt to be working with such a fine Christian couple. John and Jennifer didn't have any children of their own...at least biologically speaking. But God had blessed them with twenty-eight kids that they absolutely adored, and the feeling was mutual. The children felt loved, and it showed. Some of them had lost their parents tragically, and many others had simply been abandoned. It was amazing how God could turn heartache into triumph. The Hawks took this mission to their heart and watered it with love and compassion. A couple from the church they attend had agreed to oversee the children so that John and Jennifer could come to the dinner. Their love for the kids was very obvious, but Sarah had thought for some time that they needed a break, and it seemed that Mary had also noticed the tired lines in their faces.

Elizabeth had mentioned that her brother would be back in town and would also be in attendance at the dinner. Sarah felt a knot of nerves in her stomach at the thought of any discussion concerning baseball. She had very little experience with the sport...or any sport for that matter. Her life had always been about Band-Aids and cotton balls, not ball bats and baseballs. Oh, well. If the conversation was not in her favor, she had no problem with simply being a good listener. She pulled up to the garage and made her way to the side entrance to slip up the back stairway that came out right beside Mr. Patrick's room. She would go and check on him before joining the others. She had hoped that Mr. Patrick would feel up to coming down to dinner, but Mary had called to let her know he would not be joining their party and asked if she could check in on him from time to time during the evening. Knowing she was running late, Sarah quickly climbed the stairs and opened the door, only to collide hard with something...or someone.

Dave was back. Elizabeth was excited that he was going to be home for the dinner party. Her mom had only invited a few friends...the Hawks, the Martins, Sarah, and of course, Steve. She was sort of glad that her mom hadn't gone all out with the invitations. She knew Dave longed for some peace, which a large crowd definitely would not provide. The final list tallied around six guests, all good friends of her parents. She knew the motive of the dinner...to draw her dad out of the state of depression he had gotten himself into. Unfortunately, he had flatly refused to come down and that had done nothing to lift her mother's spirits, so she was trying to be extra positive and get her mother's mind off of her failed mission. Maria began serving the hors d'oeuvres as the guests began milling into the great room. It was wonderful to see Dave. He looked completely relaxed in his Dockers and burgundy shirt with the sleeves rolled up, holding his soda and talking to

Steve and John. John had been one of Dave's few close friends who truly cared and prayed for him, and Steve was considered family. Suddenly, Elizabeth heard a commotion as she spotted Mr. and Mrs. Martin coming through the entryway with their niece, Elsie. She knew that the invitation to the Martins had not included extended family members. Elsie Martin was here for one reason and one reason only…Dave. She tried to rescue her brother by moving over to where he was standing and giving him warning before Mrs. Martin could strike, but…too late.

"Why, Dave! I didn't know you'd be back from Atlanta in time to be here tonight!"

Elizabeth rolled her eyes and crossed her arms, thinking to herself, *Yeah, right.*

"Do you remember my niece, Elsie? She's home from college for a few days, and I couldn't just leave her home alone. So, I decided to bring her along."

Elizabeth stepped over to the foursome. "Oh! I thought Elsie was surely old enough to stay home alone."

Dave couldn't help but chuckle. But Mrs. Martin was undaunted. She looked around the room, completely disregarding Elizabeth's presence and her comment. "I see there aren't any other young people here, so maybe the two of you could be a couple for the evening."

Elizabeth to the rescue! "Oh, I'm sorry Mrs. Martin, but Dave is helping keep an eye on Dad tonight." Then she turned to Dave where the two women couldn't see her face as she winked. "I think you probably need to go ahead and check on him."

With a grateful look to his sister, who he thought was the most wonderful woman in the world at that moment, he excused himself before making a hasty exit to the second floor.

"Yes, that's a good idea." He handed his soda to Elizabeth with a wink. "Excuse me, ladies."

David could hear Mrs. Martin calling from behind him. "Maybe Elsie could help. She's had first aid, you know." But he never broke stride as he made his way out of the great room and into the foyer.

Elizabeth made small talk with Elsie to keep her from offering any *help* with their father as excuse to stay in Dave's company. She was all too familiar with the lowest of the low female tactics.

While listening to Mrs. Martin gush about all of Elsie's accomplishments, Elizabeth wondered where in the world Sarah was. She must have gotten held up at the office and was running late. She had come to the rescue of her brother, but now she waited to be rescued herself. She knew Sarah well enough to know that she would help her make a tactful retreat from this tenacious man-hunter. As Mrs. Martin rattled on and on, Elizabeth's patience began to run thin. *Sarah, I don't know where you are, but please hurry before I knock this woman over the head with something!*

Dave made his retreat to the second floor. When he entered his father's room, he was sleeping soundly. The only light was a little night-light beside the private bathroom door. He sank down into the chair at the bedside and heaved a long, heavy sigh, resting his head on the winged-back chair and stretching his long legs out in front of him. The thought of returning for dinner made his stomach churn. It was unsettling to know that he was not even safe in his own home, but he would try to make the best of it for his mother's sake. She always enjoyed dinner parties and especially looked forward to the company. He was looking forward to meeting Dad's new doctor and asking a few questions. This Dr. Phillips must be really something if Mom was inviting him to dinner after such a short acquaintance. At least John and Jennifer had been able to come, and he had enjoyed a few minutes of conversation with his friend. But Elsie Martin. He remembered meeting her about a year ago. He had not been impressed then and he was less impressed now. She dressed in a way that brought unflattering attention and her mannerisms yelled, "I'm shallow and selfish." He knew he had to go back downstairs, but who knows how many more of his mom's friends decided to come and bring their sister, niece, or cousin. He slowly rose from the chair and walked to the back staircase, knowing that taking the long way around would delay his meeting with yet another female. With his head down, feeling frustrated and disgusted he reached for the door when...*wham!* Right in the head!

David staggered backward and pressed a hand to his forehead as he caught a watery-eyed glimpse of a young woman coming through the door. Someone had obviously directed her to where he was with absolutely no regard for him or his father's privacy. This was too much. He refused to be captive in his own home. There would be no more hiding and retreating from his own living room. He felt his blood pressure rising as he fought for control of his emotions, knowing he was about to put this matter to rest once and for all. Surely this was a friend or relative of one of Mom's guests, and he didn't want to disrespect his mother, but it had gone too far. He could feel his jaw clench.

"Where do you think you're going?" He was wincing and looking more at the floor than at her.

"I-I'm s-so sorry. I..."

"Look. I know why you're here. You probably made some sweet little comment about coming up here and helping Dad, when what you really wanted was a chance to flirt with me. I can't believe what you women will stoop to. When will you ever learn that men are not looking for tramps? Quit throwing yourself at men and have a little self-respect. And tell all your little man-hunting friends that if any of you weasel your way into my house again, I'll have a police escort waiting for you the minute you set foot on the property."

The initial sting from his wallop on the head had eased, and he dropped his hand from his forehead to settle them on his hips along with a long sigh as he steadied his gaze on an absolute lovely face...stunned, but lovely. She had long, blond hair that wisped around her shoulders and the most clear and honest blue eyes he had ever seen. They were like a deep mountain lake. He had seen lots of pretty women, but this was sweet loveliness. How could this beautiful woman bring herself to such abasement?

Suddenly, Maria, who had come up the main staircase, was padding up behind him.

"There you are, Dr. Phillips! Mrs. Patrick was getting worried about you. Will you be coming down soon?"

Until now, Sarah had stood in stunned silence, but Maria's presence had helped to pull her from the haze of utter disbelief of what had just happened. Her throat was dry, and the words were slow and hoarse. She slowly looked over at Maria and addressed her in Spanish. "Uh...I need to check on Mr. Patrick before I come down. I won't be long."

Before Maria turned to relay her message to Mrs. Patrick, she looked at David. "You know your mother will want you to come down soon, too. So, don't be long."

But David didn't even acknowledge the request. He just stood staring at Sarah. *This is Dr. Phillips?! Why had no one cared to mention the fact that she was a she? Or that she was a twenty-something bombshell!* His brain just froze as to what to do or say next.

The short conversation with Maria had brought Sarah back to the world of reality. She hadn't been in the States for very long, but long enough to understand the reputation of American athletes. Arrogant, self-serving, and loose were just a few adjectives that came to mind. How could this man standing before her be even remotely related to Jack, Mary, and Elizabeth? She loved this family, but his behavior was something she just couldn't ignore. He had challenged her Christian testimony and her reputation, and she wasn't about to let this egotistical jerk get away with such outrageous allegations.

"So you're David Patrick."

Up until this point, Sarah had been a few feet away, but she stepped closer with ease and absolute control to look up into his eyes with an undeniable fire in her own. With her voice cool and steady, she meant to refute all accusations.

David swiped a hand down his jaw. "Ma'am…I-I'm sor—"

Sarah interrupted. "Mrs. Patrick has secured my services as physician to your father. It looks like we may be seeing one another from time to time, so there are a few things that I believe you should know, Mr. Patrick. First, I'm a Christian. I accepted Jesus Christ as my savior many years ago, and he's been a faithful guide in my life ever since. I *never* want to do anything that would bring shame on his name. I agree that some women do lower themselves to be what they think is attractive to lewd men, but I can assure you that I am *not* one of them. There's not a man on Earth that I would compromise my testimony or reputation for. By the grace of God, I will never stoop to such base and common behavior."

She stepped closer, almost nose to nose if her height would have allowed. David's chest tightened as he smelled her flowery perfume and looked into her clear, blue eyes. She was gorgeous. But she was also angry, and she had a right to be. Her self-control was amazing. Her words were slow and deliberate.

"So, let's get this straight with no mistake. I'm here as a guest of your mother, a friend to your sister, physician to your father, and *nothing* to you. That's where it begins and ends, Mr. Patrick."

She stood staring hard into his eyes for a moment before she stepped around him and swept into his father's bedroom to check her patient. David Patrick was left standing speechless in the hallway.

Chapter Six

After Sarah stepped into the dim light of her patient's room, she sat down in the chair at the bedside trying to recover her emotions. She felt weak, and her head was spinning from the rush of anger. How dare that man accuse her of such behavior! He had no right. He didn't even know her! She was still trembling when she looked down at Jack, sleeping soundly in his bed. Her thoughts went to the other members of the family, whom she had come to love and appreciate over the last few days. What would happen now? Would this pompous son of theirs send her packing? Well, she couldn't worry about that now. What was done was done, and she certainly wouldn't take back a single word she had said. She was thankful that God had helped her defend her testimony with calm demeanor, but it seemed that the dinner that she had looked so forward to was going to be…well…very awkward, at best. After checking Mr. Patrick's vitals, she made her way downstairs, knowing that it would be hard to swallow a single bite.

As she approached the dining room, the tinkling of silver could be heard along with a low hum of conversation. Dinner had already begun, which meant that her entrance would seem intrusive and, therefore, embarrassing. The fact that David Patrick would be watching her make a spectacle of herself made her want to get back in her car and drive home. Why she should care what he thought, she didn't know. Standing in the dim light of the great room, she was able to observe the dining room and assess the most tactful moment to enter. Obviously, the prayer had already been offered, so slipping in while heads were bowed wasn't an option. She took a deep breath and stepped one foot toward the door, when Maria came into the other end of the dining room from the kitchen, carrying a large serving tray loaded with delicious appetizers for the hungry guests. Every eye was focused on Maria and away from Sarah's side of the room so that her entrance went practically unnoticed. Except by Elizabeth, who sat close to the door and had saved her a seat. As she quickly slipped into her chair, she rolled a look to her friend and mouthed a grateful, "Thank you."

But unfortunately, it didn't take Mary long to see the new addition to the table. "Sarah! I'm glad you could make it! I was getting worried about you."

Oh, well. So much for being unnoticed. "Y-Yes, ma'am. I apologize for being late."

Mary was smiling her sweetest smile. It was her gift of hospitality that made people feel welcome and comfortable, no matter the circumstances.

"That's quite all right, dear. I'm sure you've had a busy day. We're just beginning the meal. I'm glad you're here." Mary looked around the table. "This is Jack's doctor, Sarah Phillips. Sarah, let me introduce everyone. Of course, you know John and Jennifer. And this is Robert and Martha Martin, along with Robert's niece, Elsie. Beside Elsie is Steve Travis...and I don't believe you've met my son, David."

Since slipping into her chair beside Elizabeth, she had been chatting to her friend and making apology for her tardiness. Sarah hadn't noticed that David was sitting directly in front of her. She felt her face flush at the sight of him. His gaze steadied on her, with his handsome dark eyes. He didn't seem angry. On the contrary, there was a softness about him, and something in that look that shook her just a little. She gathered her nerves and attempted to sweep a smile and slight nod across to each guest. "I'm pleased to meet all of you."

Maria set a bowl of soup, along with a small biscuit in front of her. She spoke a polite "gracias" to Maria and lowered her head, concentrating on the soup and trying desperately hard not to look across the table. She could feel his stare, and it unnerved her completely. *Come on, Sarah, don't let this guy get to you. Remember, he puts his boots on one at a time, like everyone else.* Her thoughts were interrupted by Mr. Martin.

"Dr. Phillips? Mary tells us that you were a missionary in Honduras before coming to America. I visited that part of the world several years ago. In what part of the country did you live?"

David put down his fork and folded his hands as he propped his elbows on the table in interest. *She had been a missionary in Central America?*

"I lived near the town of Olanchito, in the northern plains. My parents and four siblings still live there."

"And your father is a doctor too?"

"Yes, sir. That's correct."

"You're awfully young. How long have you been a doctor?"

Sarah smiled. "It seems like my whole life. I began helping my father when I was eleven."

"Eleven! You're kidding?"

She shrugged one shoulder. "He needed an assistant, and I was the oldest, so I got the job. But officially speaking, I've been a doctor for almost eight months now."

Mrs. Martin was getting perturbed with her husband's attention toward this pretty dinner guest. She interrupted with more accolades for Elsie. "Mary, did I tell you that Elsie has been taking piano lessons? She is really quite accomplished for one who has only been taking lessons for such a short time. And did I tell you…"

David had completely tuned out whatever gibberish Mrs. Martin was spouting about her silly niece and was staring at the woman sitting directly across from him. She was amazingly beautiful in the candlelit dining room. Her blue dress made her blue eyes shine all the more, and her hair was like spun gold. He had never been so impressed with someone that he had just met.

She was kind, intelligent, poised, and elegant. It had not escaped his attention that she had spoken to Maria several times in Spanish during the course of the evening. When speaking to Mr. Martin about assisting her father since age eleven, she had brushed it off as no big deal. She was so comfortable with who she was that she didn't care who was impressed or who wasn't. How could he have gotten on unfriendly terms with this woman? No…this lady.

Everyone finished their dessert and filed back into the great room for coffee. Dave and John stood talking over by the fireplace, while Elizabeth sat on the sofa with Elsie, not wanting to exclude her guest and trying to make small talk. Sarah walked over to the far end of the room to talk with Jennifer, and Steve had settled into a chair in the far corner to enjoy his coffee.

Everyone seemed content and relaxed in their own conversation until Mrs. Martin spotted the grand piano in the corner and announced, "While we have our coffee, it would be a perfect time for Elsie to play a piece on the piano!" Mrs. Martin began to wave her arms impatiently for Elsie to come. "Come, dear, and play that new one you've been working on…unless, of course, someone else would like to play." Turning to Sarah she asked, "Doctor, do you play the piano?"

Sarah had discerned the woman's reason for asking. It seemed to be a deliberate attempt to belittle her and make her niece look good. This was a common tactic among silly women. "My sister is the pianist in my family. She plays beautifully."

Mrs. Martin glanced at Dave. "Oh. That's too bad. Every cultured young lady should be musically inclined."

Sarah replied, "Yes, ma'am," then turned to continue her conversation with Jennifer, as if she couldn't care less what this shallow woman thought.

Mrs. Martin looked impatiently at Elsie. "Well, play, dear!"

She began to play a tune that was completely unrecognizable. The sour notes definitely outnumbered the good ones. As Sarah watched her try to get through the song, she suddenly felt rather sorry for Elsie. She was really not a bad sort, just the victim of poor training and bad advice. Her aunt had somehow convinced her that being silly and showy would win her some attention from a proper suitor…namely David. She was getting attention all right, but not the kind she intended.

Much to the relief of everyone, the song was finally over. Mrs. Martin jumped to her feet and began clapping wildly. She looked over at Mary. "Wasn't that wonderful?!"

Mary, wanting to be the gracious hostess, slowly shook her head with a sheepish grin. "It was like nothing I've ever heard."

Mrs. Martin looked at Dave excitedly. "What did you think, Dave?"

Taken off guard by the question, Dave practically choked on his coffee. "Uh...amazing. I'm afraid I didn't recognize the piece, though. What was it?"

Mrs. Martin's excitement popped like a balloon. She responded blandly, "Amazing Grace." At which time, Steve ended up choking on his own coffee and tried to cover it with a few coughs.

Dave lifted his mug to his lips with a soft "Oh" before he took a long sip. "Well, I need to go back up and check on Dad."

Elsie stood up from the piano stool with her face puckered. "I thought that was Sarah's job! After all, she is the doctor, isn't she?"

Sarah looked at David half smiling, knowing that he was just trying to make an escape. "She's right, it is my job. I can go check on him."

But David was not going to be denied. If Elsie played one more tune, he was sure that every dog within ten miles would join in chorus. "That's all right. You stay and enjoy some time with Jennifer." And before anyone could protest, he was striding out of the room.

Robert Martin stood and rubbed his tummy. "Mary, that sure was a good dinner. But if I don't get home soon, I'll be sound asleep in front of this warm fire, and you'll all have to listen to me snore the rest of the evening. Martha, let's head home."

Martha and Elsie shot a frustrated look at poor Robert. "But, Robert, the night's young, and we can't leave without saying good-bye to David! It would be rude."

Elizabeth to the rescue again! "That's all right, Mrs. Martin. I'll tell David good-bye for you." She put an arm around Mrs. Martin and began guiding her to the door. "I'm sure he'll understand. Besides, he may be with Dad for quite some time." They made it to the foyer, and Elizabeth grabbed her guest's coat and eased it around her shoulders. "If Dad's awake, he likes for Dave to stay and talk for a while. You understand." Reluctantly, they said their good-byes and headed out into the chilly night air.

Mary hated to admit it, but she was more relaxed now that they were gone. If she had known that Martha had planned such a coordinated attack on her son, she certainly would have never invited them. But Jack really liked Robert and so did she. He was such a patient man, but then...he *had* to be.

Elizabeth came back to take her place beside the fire. Steve, who was sipping his coffee, sat down beside her on the hearth and gave a low, inconspicuous chuckle. "Dave will owe you *big* for that one."

Liz picked up her coffee mug and gave him a knowing grin. "Yes, he will. And I'm counting on you to remind him of it on a regular basis." They softly clinked their coffee cups.

Chapter Seven

David sat down in the same chair he had sunk down into just two short hours ago—and for the same reason…to avoid a female. This had been a roller coaster ride of an evening. How could this have happened? In all his conversations with Elizabeth, she never mentioned that their dad's doctor was a beautiful, Christian, young lady from the mission field. And why did he care? He had seen pretty faces before. It was like he had built-up immunity to all the superficial gloss. But this was different. *She* was different. For the first time in a long time, there was someone who didn't care who he was. This girl had grit. She didn't put on an act to get his attention. She stood firmly on who and what she was with unwavering tenacity. He had a feeling that if the president of the United States had implied that she was a tramp, he would have promptly received the same speech. She was confident but not arrogant. Beautiful but not flirtatious. Intelligent but not condescending.

He was pulled from his thoughts as Mr. Patrick began to stir from beneath the covers. David stepped over to the bedside.

"Dad, are you okay?"

He tried to mumble something, but David couldn't understand. Maybe something was wrong. He needed to get the doctor. David made his way back down the stairs just in time to see Maria close the door behind Robert Martin. At least that worry was off his mind. He could go back into the room without the fear of another attack by Martha and Elsie. But the thought of facing Sarah wrenched his stomach into a hundred knots. What must she think of him? Well, he couldn't think about that right now. As uncomfortable as it was going to be to speak to her again, his dad needed help. He quietly slipped over to Sarah, who was still standing in the corner talking to Jennifer.

"Excuse me, Doctor. Dad woke up, and I think he needs something, but I can't understand him. Would you mind coming upstairs?"

"Oh, of course. Excuse me, Jennifer."

She understood David's hushed tones; he didn't want to disturb his mother. They quietly slipped out of the room and into the foyer while Mary's back was turned.

David looked apologetic. "I'm sorry to have to pull you away."

The concern clouded her face. "That's quite all right. I'm glad you did."

Side by side they climbed the stairs. It had not escaped Sarah's attention of how handsome David was. With his dark hair, rich brown eyes, shadowy stubble on his strong face and muscular build, she could understand Elsie's desire to attract his attention. But she had no such desire herself. Good looks were only skin deep. She had always been very practical about such matters. After all, it was what was on the inside that really counted, right? Right. But she did have regret that David was unlike his parents and sister because she sure could spend a lifetime looking at him. She took a deep breath and looked away. That was dangerous thinking, and she couldn't allow it to invade her thoughts. This is the man that, just a few short hours ago, had accused her of being a tramp. It just didn't make sense. She knew John and Jennifer well, and they both seemed to think so highly of him. Maybe they hadn't seen the side of David that she had the misfortune of seeing. Well, she would clear her mind of him once and for all. Yes, he had behaved abominably, but out of her care for Jack, Mary and Elizabeth, she could be civil. She was here to care for his father, and that was it. She had to stay focused and professional. Mr. Patrick's health depended on it. They climbed each step in awkward silence until she finally spoke, keeping her head down and her eyes on the steps.

"Mr. Patrick, I know you've only been home for a short time, but can you tell me how your father has been doing during the day? You see, I'm only here in the evenings."

David looked concerned. "Well, mostly he's been doing nothing. He just wants to stay under the covers and sleep as much as possible. He says very little to any of us. I confess that I haven't talked to him very much. It's kind of embarrassing, not being able to understand him. Dad and I have always been close, but now we can't even carry on a simple conversation."

Sarah appreciated the fact that he cared so much for his parents. "I can understand that. But the more you talk to him, the better it will be for the both of you. It will help improve his speech and help you understand him better. I'm afraid that he's slipping into a deep depression. It's typical of stroke patients…especially ones that were previously very active. It's important that we stop that from happening. He needs fresh air and sunshine in the worst sort of way. While the weather is still mild, I plan to get him out to enjoy it first thing tomorrow."

They reached the second floor. David looked at her with narrowed eyes. "But tomorrow's Saturday. Isn't it your day off?"

Her lips lifted into a beautiful smile, and her blue eyes twinkled. "I'm never off, Mr. Patrick."

He was amazed with how at ease she was with him. There didn't seem to be any anger or animosity on her part, even though he knew she had a right to be upset with him. Neither was she in the least bit intimidated. It was as though she had put the whole episode from the hallway behind her. She was completely focused on the task at hand. He knew had an apology to make…a big one. But where did he begin to explain? And would she even understand if he did? He wasn't sure what to say, but he definitely wanted to be on friendly terms.

When they entered the dimly lit room, Jack was trying to sit up. Sarah walked quickly over to him, hoping to steady him into position before he tumbled to the floor.

"There, Mr. Patrick. Are you comfortable?"

The muddled reply came back. "Baaaa...ooo."

Sarah could see the desperation in his eyes as he tried to make her understand.

"Baaaa.....oooooooo!" This time with more intensity.

Her face broke into a smile. "Oh! You need to go to the bathroom?"

His face instantly relaxed as he slowly nodded his head.

"Well, I think that can be arranged. I brought your son along with me. He can help, okay?"

He gave another nod with a little crooked smile.

Sarah threw back the covers, walked over to open the bathroom door, and turned on the light.

She looked over at David. "All right, Mr. Patrick. If you can just help me steady him, I think we'll make it just fine."

With one on either side, they gently lifted him to his feet. The right foot was dragging a bit, but David was able to compensate and pull him along, bearing the brunt of the weight. Sarah waited outside the door until the two reappeared, and she caught Jack's arm to lead him back to the bed. After he was situated in a propped-up position, she pulled up the little winged-back chair to the bedside and employed her very cheeriest but soft disposition. David stood back in the shadow of the room and watched her interact with his dad. She was obviously trying to pull him out of his solemn mood. And judging by his reaction, it was working. David smiled to himself. If a beautiful woman like Sarah pulled up a chair to talk to him, it would definitely put *him* in a good mood.

"I'm sorry you had to wait for so long." She smiled. "We need to give you something like a bell to ring when you need us." Then she chuckled. "No. I've got it...an air horn. You know, like the one Elizabeth has. I had never seen one until she snuck up behind me the other day and blew that crazy thing. I nearly jumped through the roof!"

She leaned over and softened her voice as if sharing a secret. "Just between you and me, I think she's got a mean streak in her.

Now, who do you suppose she gets that from?" Jack wrinkled up a smile and looked at his son.

David, who was standing in the corner with his arms crossed over his broad chest, had a surprised look on his face. Sarah leaned back into the chair as she started laughing out loud. "I think you must be right. He looks completely guilty to me." And for the first time in nearly four weeks, Jack Patrick let out a soft chuckle.

Sarah made small talk for a few more minutes as she conversed with him about the weather and various other light subjects. Then her tone slightly changed. But it was very subtle, and she kept a soft smile on her lips.

"I was disappointed that you didn't come down to dinner tonight. Mrs. Mary sure knows how to throw a party. I was pleased to meet your friends, Robert and Martha Martin. They also had their niece, Elsie, with them, and I met David's friend, Steve. God has blessed you with some great friends."

David fully expected his dad to retreat back into his shell, but to his amazement, he just kept looking at Sarah. He was totally comfortable with her. The frustration and irritability that he had demonstrated in the last few weeks was completely gone. This lovely little missionary doctor had won his total trust. She took his hand in hers and gently rubbed it with her thumb.

"Mr. Patrick, I know that you may feel uncomfortable being in front of other people right now, but you have to believe that this is only temporary. You're already making great progress. Mary loves you so much, and it would mean a great deal to her if you would come down, even if for just a short time." Her manner was easy and nonthreatening. She wasn't pressuring him at all but was giving him back his independence in his right to choose.

David cocked one eyebrow. His dad was a proud man and would never consent to facing the world in this condition. But he didn't seem to be resisting the idea either. He was quietly studying her face.

Sarah could read Jack's expression. He was giving the matter serious thought, so she kept talking. "The Martins just left, which only leaves Steve, John, and Jennifer, and they're practically family. David can help you into your chair and take you down in the service elevator if you like. Would you allow him to do that?"

He just looked at her until she cocked her head to one side and raised her eyebrows to ask, "Please?" David could see his father's face relax as he slowly nodded his consent.

Sarah had succeeded in melting Jack's heart. And in that moment, she was melting another heart in the room as well.

Chapter Eight

Sarah threw back the covers again and, noticing his pajamas, walked over to the closet to pull out a clean robe. She helped him slide into the sleeves, and David stepped over to pick up his dad. But Sarah put her hand on his arm. "Wait." She disappeared into the bathroom, and the two men heard her rattling around in one of the drawers until she reappeared with a brush in her hand.

Sarah walked over to Jack and smiled as she tilted his face toward her and began smoothing his hair into style. "I saw a gorgeous lady downstairs so we had better get you dolled up. Her name is Mary, and I think she'll really go for you." Her teasing got another soft chuckle.

Sarah stood and leaned back to observe her handiwork. "Yes. That's much better." She nodded at David and moved out of the way. She was amazed at the ease with which he scooped his father into his arms and gently placed him in the wheelchair.

After grabbing a small blanket, she whisked out the door and was waiting in the foyer when Jack and David arrived. Wrapped in his silk black robe with the blanket draped over his legs, he looked quite distinguished.

Mary's back was turned to the door when David wheeled Jack into the great room. She could tell that something was going on by the expressions on all the faces looking over her shoulder. She slowly turned around. Jack was trying to curve his lips into a smile. The emotion was overwhelming, but she kept herself under control. Jack wouldn't want her to make a spectacle. It was all she could do to keep from bursting into tears and throwing her arms around him. All smiles, she walked over to him and leaned over to place a soft kiss on his lips. She pressed her cheek to his and whispered, "I'm so glad you came. I love you, Jack." With tears in her eyes, she looked up at Sarah and mouthed, "Thank you."

Sarah leaned over to Jack's other ear and, with a twinkle in her eye, looked over at Mary. "See, I knew she'd really go for you."

David just stood, holding onto the handles of the wheelchair, watching the scene. His conscience chided him for the mistake he had made. It was obvious that this woman had been a ray of sunshine to his family. She had been recommended by John and Jennifer, which meant that she had not in any way "weaseled her way into his home," as he had previously suggested to her face. His heart ached at the thought of the scene in the hallway. All he could do now is pray that he could apologize soon and hope she would understand. But women hold grudges. They all do. And he figured this one was no different. David could feel the resentment of past experiences rising up. But as he looked at Sarah, there was something knocking at his heart that told him he was wrong to think that about this lady. Her obvious care for his family and the way she had treated him with respect, in spite of his vicious attack on her character, told him otherwise. She was gentle, thoughtful, and hopefully...forgiving.

John walked over to speak to Jack, but when he reached out his hand for a shake, he realized that Jack couldn't respond. Sarah had always appreciated John's tact. He was a true gentleman all the way. He lifted Jack's hand to his own in such a way that seemed completely natural and gave it a hearty shake.

"It's great to see you, Jack!"

Steve watched John's reaction to Jack's limp hand and decided to give a nod instead of a handshake as his greeting. "Jack."

Jennifer walked up behind her husband and laid a hand on Jack's arm with a warm smile.

"We've had a wonderful evening, and we really appreciate you and Mrs. Mary inviting us. I'm glad you could join the party."

Jack had never been one who enjoyed the spotlight, and David knew that his dad would feel more at ease if he moved everyone's focus to something else. He wheeled the chair into position near the fireplace and then gave attention to his friend.

"Hey! John. How about a song?"

John laughed. "Come on, Dave. You don't want to put everybody through that kind of agony, do you?"

Mary chimed in. "Please, John. You have such a wonderful voice. Sing my favorite!"

Finally, John consented. "Well, okay, but only on one condition…if Sarah agrees to accompany me."

Sarah's eyes widened as John walked over to the fireplace. "Jack, do you still have that guitar of yours?"

Jack nodded, and Mary shot out of her chair to retrieve it from a nearby closet.

Jennifer took the arm of a very reluctant Sarah and escorted her to the hearth. "Oh, yes! Sarah plays the guitar beautifully!"

Sarah slowly sat down on the hearth as Mary presented her with the guitar. She was wondering what Mrs. Patrick's favorite song was, and hoping on top of hope that she could play it with no music and no practice. John stepped over beside her and leaned down to whisper, "'He Hideth My Soul.' In the key of C, please."

Her hands glided over the strings as she began the introduction, followed by John's rich baritone.

"A wonderful savior is Jesus, my Lord. A wonderful savior to me. He hideth my soul in the cleft of the Rock, where rivers of pleasure I see."

The room was filled with the peaceful presence of the Lord. When John reached the chorus, Sarah gave the music a proper crescendo to give accent to the power of the words.

"He hideth my soul in the cleft of the rock that shadows a dry, thirsty land. He hideth my life in the depths of his love and covers me there with His hand, and covers me there with His hand."

When the last note died, no one spoke for a moment. Finally, Mary, who was wiping her eyes, broke the silence. "Thank you, John. Sarah, that was beautiful."

Elizabeth came over to sit beside Sarah on the hearth in front of the warm crackling fire and gave her friend a soft, friendly punch on the shoulder.

"Why didn't you tell me you play the guitar?"

Sarah gave her a teasing grin. "You never asked me."

Elizabeth knew that Sarah had never enjoyed great wealth and had been very limited in opportunity, having lived in such a poor country for most of her life. And yet she played with such expertise and feeling.

"How in the world did you learn to play so well?"

Sarah was very reluctant when it came to speaking about her personal talents and abilities, so it was Jennifer who chimed in.

"All of Sarah's family is musically gifted in several instruments. Piano, guitar, violin…"

Elizabeth's interest was piqued. "So how did you learn?"

Sarah knew Elizabeth was not going to let this go without explanation.

"My father was rarely paid with money. People simply traded what they could for his services. Chickens, cloth, canned goods…. There was one man in particular who repaired instruments. Whenever my father's services were needed, he would be paid with an instrument each time. So, we had a variety of different ones."

Elizabeth still looked confused. "Yes, but how did you learn to play them?"

Sarah chuckled. "When you don't have a television, and the only entertainment you have is what you make for yourself, you learn to make do with what you have. So, when another instrument was brought home, we would all gather around to try and figure it out. With no instruction manual, it was quite a challenge, but I'm sure my mother appreciated it since it kept us occupied and out of trouble for hours." She rose to take the guitar back over to Mary.

"It really is a beautiful instrument. Thank you for letting me play it."

"Oh, you're welcome, dear. I hope you'll play again, sometime."

John looked at his watch. "Well, I guess we need to relieve the babysitters."

Jennifer glanced at her own wrist. "Oh, my! It *is* getting late."

Mary rose to see her guests to the door. "I'm glad you were able to come."

Jennifer gave her a warm hug. "Thank you for inviting us. It's been such a relaxing evening. We had a wonderful time."

John spoke his good-byes to Jack, Elizabeth, and Sarah. Then, he stepped over to give Dave and Steve a hearty handshake, and Mary a big, bear hug. "Mrs. Mary you outdid yourself tonight. The meal was wonderful!"

As John and Jennifer were saying their good-byes, Sarah noticed that Jack was beginning to look rather tired and worn. She asked David if he would take him back to his room, and she would come to check on him before leaving. When Jack and David left the room, Sarah said good-bye to Mary and Elizabeth. It had been a most enjoyable evening, and she had come to greatly value their friendship even more.

David rolled his father back through the kitchen and into the service elevator. By the time they reached the bedroom, and Mr. Patrick was securely in his bed, he was sound asleep in no time. As Sarah made her way to the second floor, she dreaded being with David again in close quarters. Thankfully, the evening had provided constant diversion, and she had not been forced to make conversation with him. She was so confused, her head ached. How could a man with such great family and friends be so nasty and rude? She had caught a glimpse of him after John's song and saw that he had been deeply moved. He was incredibly handsome, no doubt about it. And if the episode in the hallway had never happened, she would really like the guy. But no way could she let that happen. There was more to him than she could figure out, so she just kept repeating to herself a verse that her mother had made her learn as a child: Keep thy heart with all diligence; for out of it are the issues of life (Proverbs 4:23).

David sat in his father's room for a third time. He had to make things right with Dr. Phillips. He couldn't let her think what she must be thinking. Of the previous mental list that he had made of her attributes, he would now have to add "musically gifted" to the list. He would love to ask her to dinner. Get to know her better. But that was out of the question now. He rested his face in his hands until he heard her enter the room. She quickly moved past him to examine her patient, who seemed to be very content in his world of sleep.

She reached to feel of his hand and whispered, "I'm glad he's sleeping well. His hand feels a bit cool, though. Do you know where an extra blanket might be?"

David rose from his chair. "I think there's one in the bathroom linen closet." He walked into the big bathroom to retrieve the blanket. He knew this was the moment of truth. His heart quickened and his stomach knotted. The sooner he could make amends for his actions, the sooner he could get that dinner date. He was going to apologize and explain everything. He couldn't let the evening end like this. Tucking the blanket under his arm, he walked back into the bedroom, and…she was gone.

He strode quickly to the door and looked both ways down the hall. No Sarah. He turned back into the room and began tucking the blanket around his father, his mind reeling. *Lord, I don't know how this happened. Is this woman as real as she seems? Please give me understanding in what I should do.*

Tucking in the last corner, he felt someone's presence. He looked up to see Elizabeth with her arms crossed, leaning against the doorframe. He was unsure how long she had been standing there watching him frantically stuff the blanket under the mattress. He only hoped that in his frustration he had not been speaking his thoughts aloud. Not that he needed to. His sister had a knack for reading him like a book.

She whispered. "Getting Dad tucked in for the night?"

"Yep." David kept struggling with the covers, even though they were already perfect. He hoped that if he looked busy, she would move on. It didn't work.

Elizabeth chuckled. "You know, you're just like Mom. When something's bothering you, you work like a bee on steroids."

He muttered, "Nothing's bothering me," and kept stuffing the blanket.

Now Elizabeth was laughing hard but covered her mouth, so not to wake her father.

"Oh, yeah? Then why are you punching that blanket like you were Sylvester Stallone? Besides, you can stop now. I think it's dead."

David hated how transparent he was to his sister. He punched one more time and stood back with his hands on his hips, as if observing his handiwork, so he wouldn't have to look her in the eye. If he ever looked at her, she would see straight through him, and he couldn't afford that right now.

"There. I think he'll be comfortable now."

Elizabeth chuckled. "Yeah. He'll be comfortable unless he has to go to the bathroom during the night. In which case, we'll have to pry him out of there with a crowbar."

David ignored her teasing, hoping she would go on to bed. She didn't.

"I was wondering what you thought of Sarah?"

David didn't even want to hear that name. He had made a royal mess and was desperately trying to figure out how to fix it. If Elizabeth knew what he had done, she would hit the roof. Lost in his thoughts, he made no answer.

Elizabeth came in the room, keeping her voice low.

"Well?" She waved a hand in front of his face. "Hello? Earth to Dave."

He gave her a brotherly look of irritation and shrugged one shoulder. "She's fine."

"Fine?"

"Yeah, fine. What do you want me to say?"

A broad smile stretched across her face. "You like her, don't you?" It sounded more like a statement than a question.

He rolled his eyes and looked away, not wanting her to see the truth.

"Elizabeth, come on."

She swayed out of the room. "Okay, I'll go." Then she peaked back around the door at him with a teasing smile, as she wiggled her eyebrows up and down. "But you *do* like her."

He gave her a stern, "Good night, Elizabeth."

Chapter Nine

On Sunday, Sarah began her drive to the Valley Chapel Church where Dr. and Mrs. Barlow attended. Mrs. Carol had invited her last week during one of her cookie runs to the office, and she had promised to visit this Sunday. As Sarah drove down the little country road, she was thinking of how much she had enjoyed her Saturday visit with the Patrick's. The dread of seeing David again after the Friday night dinner party had dissipated, after learning that he was not at home but at a team meeting. Maria had helped her transport Mr. Patrick to the back patio. It had been a perfect day of warm sunshine and blue sky, and she smiled as she remembered his excitement when he used his walker for the first time to cross the lawn. The physical therapist, Mrs. Chapman, had been doing a great job but had limited his movements to inside the house, up and down the hallway. The change of scenery seemed to help lift his spirits tremendously, and she would have to mention it to Mrs. Chapman. His speech was still hindered but improving little by little. The "m" sound had returned to his vocabulary, which was very helpful in deciphering his phrases.

Sarah looked at the directions that Mrs. Carol had written down for her, to ???double check the next turn. She made a right onto another one lane dirt road and wrinkled her brow as she peered out the windshield. Was this right? She couldn't imagine anything being way out here in the middle of nowhere—let alone a church. There were no houses, no businesses, nothing. She rounded the next curve, and her face softened at the lovely scene. The little white country church sat all alone in a beautiful cove at the bottom of a snow-peaked Rocky Mountain. She pulled onto the graveled parking area just in time to see a boy around the age of eleven, wearing a pair of bibbed overalls and tousled blond hair, run out onto the front steps of the church. He jumped a couple of times before he was able to grab the long rope that was attached to the bell above. There were a few of the older men standing outside talking, and enjoying the unseasonable warmth. As the bell rang, they ambled inside and Sarah joined in behind them. She found the Barlow's seated near the back, waiting for her arrival. Carol spotted her and waved her over to sit with them. By the time she had taken her seat, the organ began to play the first hymn. It was, *In the Sweet By and By*, one of her favorites. The congregation was small, not over fifty people. But the sound of their voices thundered off the walls and wooden floor, blending in close harmony. It was a sweet mixture of young and old.

After the offering plate was passed, the organ continued to play, and people began turning to greet one another with a hearty handshake or hug. Sarah was sure she had shaken every hand by the end of the song and felt the warmth of their welcome. The pastor stepped up on the small platform behind the old wooden lectern to deliver his message. He looked to be around seventy years of age and stood about five-foot-three with a bald head, little round belly, and a big, broad smile. The suit he wore was dark blue and quite worn, but it seemed to fit the setting of this little congregation of believers. Nothing fancy, just a down-to-earth group of people who gathered to worship the God of heaven. Sarah felt as though she had stepped back into a simpler time, and it reminded her a great deal of the worship services she had enjoyed in Honduras. God was not impressed with big buildings, fancy clothes, or great, swelling words. After all, why would the God of the universe, who created the stars and the planets, the sun and the moon, rivers and oceans, man and woman, care about the cost of a suit? Pastor Mosbey gave a short greeting then launched into his message. He preached of heaven and hell, sin and righteousness, and the precious savior of the world, Jesus Christ. What he lacked in stature, he made up for in lung capacity. As he delivered his sermon with passion, Sarah noticed the nodding heads along with shouts of "Amen!" from the congregation.

After the final prayer, she shook every hand again as people lined the aisle to make their exit. When they reached the parking lot, she felt so refreshed in spirit. Mrs. Carol gave her a big, warm hug. "Thank you, for coming today, Sarah. I hope you enjoyed the service."

Sarah returned her hug. "Thank you both for inviting me. I felt like I was home again."

Dr. Barlow smiled. "Glad to hear it! I hope that means you'll come back again."

"Oh, yes! I certainly will."

Elizabeth clicked off her cell phone and propped her feet up on the ottoman as she settled back into the plush sofa.

"I still can't get in touch with Sarah. She said she was going to church with Dr. and Mrs. Barlow today, but it's going on one o'clock. I'm sure they've dismissed by now."

David kept his face buried in the newspaper. He hadn't mentioned what had happened between him and Sarah on Friday night. He had hoped to make an apology before now. It had been hard to keep his mind on the sermon at church. Every time he closed his eyes, he pictured a lovely lady with blond hair and blue eyes seated on the hearth in front of a warm, crackling fire, strumming the guitar. It occurred to him how much he cared what she thought of him. True, he needed to apologize no matter who she was. He had made a terrible mistake, and God had reminded him of his accountability more than once over the course of the weekend. But something else was nudging him to get on pleasant terms with Dr. Sarah Phillips. Elizabeth had already mentioned that Sarah had turned down an invitation to Sunday lunch. Now she was trying to get Sarah to come over and help trim the tree tomorrow night, but so far, her calls had not been returned. Maybe she had just been too busy…or maybe she had forgotten. But David knew better. From what his sister had told him, they talked every day and were best of friends. Sarah was clearly avoiding Elizabeth because of him, and she obviously had not told Elizabeth what had happened, or he would have gotten an earful from his sister by now. His heart hurt as he watched Elizabeth's confusion over her friend's silence. He would somehow make this right. One way or another, he would get Sarah here to help trim the tree tomorrow night, and his motives were not altogether focused on his sister. He acknowledged his own selfishness. He wouldn't mind seeing her again either. He turned another page of the paper. He hadn't read a single word but had to look the part, so no one would bother him while he was deep in thought. Now the question was how to go about it. A phone call was too impersonal. An apology this big had to be face to face. He had to see her before tomorrow evening, but how? Then an idea hit. He closed the paper and walked out of the room.

Chapter Ten

    Monday morning was crazy. The flu bug had hit with a vengeance, and both doctors had more than they could handle all day. Sarah felt like she had washed her hands a million times before lunch. But she couldn't wash her thoughts of Elizabeth. She had been giving her friend the cold shoulder, and it felt horrible. How would she ever explain? The fact was she could *never* tell Elizabeth what had happened. Elizabeth loved her brother dearly. *Lord, I don't know what to do or how to handle this, so I'm not going to do anything. I put it completely in your hands.*

Virtuous

The afternoon was just as hectic as the morning, and Sarah tended her last patient of the day. She stepped into her office and, with a long sigh, dropped into the leather office chair. She closed her eyes, thankful for the peace and quiet after a long day of cranky adults and crying babies. The digital clock on her desk read 5:05. Dr. Barlow had left just moments ago, and Millie was still in the front office, no doubt closing up for the night. The fatigue had set in, and the thoughts of going home were sweet, if lonely. Maybe she should have called and accepted Mary's offer to help trim the tree, but that sounded like a family event, and she felt sure that David would resent her presence. She began gathering her belongings and logging off the computer, when the door opened and Millie peaked in.

"Excuse me…Dr. Phillips?"

Sarah looked up. "Millie? I thought you were gone for the day."

"I'm sorry to bother you, but you have another patient."

Sarah was exhausted and rather annoyed at the late appointment. "What…now?"

"Yes, ma'am. I'm sorry, but he insisted on seeing you." Millie winked and gave Sarah a knowing look. Sarah couldn't help but be amazed at her upbeat attitude after such an exhausting day.

Sarah sighed and her lips pulled up into a tired, lopsided smile. Helping others didn't always equal convenience. "Okay, Millie. What room?"

"Room 3."

"You can go ahead and leave. I'll lock up. Thanks, Millie."

"You're welcome. 'Night, Doc."

"Good night."

Millie peaked back in with a big smile. "By the way, I got that autograph."

Sarah gave her a confused look but decided to go along with whatever Millie was saying. She didn't have the energy or concentration to decipher the meaning behind the words. All she could say was, "That's nice. 'Night."

Millie chuckled as she closed the door. "Good night."

Sarah pulled back on her lab coat, threw her stethoscope around her neck, and headed down the hall to room 3. She grabbed the chart from the door and was studying it as she turned the knob, and the door swung open to find David Patrick perched on the examining table.

Sarah caught a quick gasp when she recognized him, and her heart raced. Under the florescent light, his features were striking. He wore jeans and a black T-shirt that stretched taut across a broad chest and arms. His watch wrapped around a muscular forearm. She knew her face was flushed as the warmth crept up her neck. She looked back down at the chart. Her tired mind grasped for words, and her spirit begged for composure. A quick request for help from above whispered over her lips. When she looked up, she felt a little more in control…but not much. He didn't look sick, but he didn't look well either. His face held a soft, yet serious expression. She swallowed hard, hoping the words would come out.

She nodded and spoke a formal, "Mr. Patrick."

He cleared his throat. "Hi."

Was it her imagination, or did he seem just as nervous as she was? She took a deep breath, remembering that she was a doctor, and right now, he was her patient. Apparently, something was wrong, and it was her job to help. Composure was of the essence.

"I'm afraid your chart doesn't indicate the reason for your visit. How can I help you?"

He cleared his throat again. "It's my feet."

She looked at him concerned and a little confused. "Your feet?"

"Yes, ma'am."

She looked down at his oversized, black and gray sneakers. "What seems to be the trouble?"

"I stuck both of them in my mouth Friday night."

She slowly lifted her gaze to his handsome face, a smile flirting at the corner of her mouth as she bit her lower lip. "Oh?"

"You see, I met a very nice lady over the weekend, but I made a terrible mistake. I said some things to her that I wish I could take back. I'd like to have a chance to apologize and explain, but I don't know if she'll listen."

Sarah couldn't help but be impressed by this creative apology and decided to play along. Keeping a straight face, she hugged the clipboard and put forth her most professional manner.

"Well, I can't answer for your lady friend. But maybe it would help to try out your apology on someone else first. I'm a pretty good listener." She sat down in one of the chairs and motioned for him to sit in the chair beside her.

David hopped off the table and lowered his large frame into the chair, turning slightly toward her. He felt a bit more confident, now that he knew she wasn't going to toss him out of her office. He noticed how shocked she had been when she first entered the room, but now she was the lovely lady from the dinner party...gentle and poised. He leaned over, propping his elbows on his knees and clasping his hands together. His pulse quickened, and he breathed a deep sigh. He had prayed long and hard about this moment and rehearsed his words over and over, but now, face-to-face, he wasn't as sure of himself. *Lord, a little help please.*

Sarah knew David was handsome, but right now, he was absolutely *Wow*. It wasn't just his physique, it was the way he carried himself. His face held the same gentleness as his mother, and he didn't seem arrogant at all. In fact, he almost seemed...well...humble. He was close enough for the aroma of his woodsy aftershave to fill her senses. This was a completely different image of who she had thought him to be. Whatever he had to say, he had her undivided attention. He cleared his throat yet another time. He was clearly nervous and kept looking at the floor.

"Uh...Dr. Phillips, I owe you a big apology. I'm truly sorry for the things I said to you the other night." He finally looked up at her with his beautiful velvet brown eyes. "But I don't want to just apologize, I want you to understand why I said what I did, and I hardly know where to start."

He stopped and breathed a long sigh. Sarah could hear the sincerity in his voice. He was being so honest that she wanted to somehow comfort him and put him at ease. This man didn't only have a need to apologize. He needed someone to talk to.

She reached over and put a hand on his arm as she gave him a gentle smile. "Why don't you start by calling me Sarah."

David looked deep into her soft, blue eyes, and his heart fell to his toes. He didn't see a grudge or any spite at all. Her face was pure compassion. She wasn't going to make him crawl and beg but was giving freely of her forgiveness. There was a peace about her that gave him liberty to say what he needed in order to make things right between them.

"You see, I've had some bad experiences in the past that have made me very wary of strangers. I guess you could say I have some trust issues. Even Elizabeth has endured heartache because of me and become less trusting of people. She had what she thought was a friend a couple of years ago. As it turned out, her *friend* was only interested in getting close to me. She followed me everywhere I went." He winced and shook his head. "I don't want that to sound arrogant. It's not that I think I'm a great catch or anything, it's just that people get so caught up in sports celebrities. They make us out to be something we're not." He took a deep breath. "Anyway, when Elizabeth realized the reason for the girl's interest, she was really hurt. Liz has always looked out for me, and I feel it's my job to look out for her too. So, when I saw you coming upstairs the other night, I thought it was another situation like the last one." His face was absolute sincerity. "I'm not making excuses for what I did, I just wanted you to know the reasons."

Sarah was speechless. If true beauty was on the inside, this guy was handsome through and through. She had no experience with this kind of attraction and didn't know exactly what to do with it. She tried to clear her head.

"I really appreciate your apology, and I want you to know that I would never do anything to hurt Elizabeth. When I first moved here, I missed my sister terribly. God knew my loneliness, and I believe he gave me a true friend in Elizabeth." She smiled. "The Lord will do that, you know." Her expression became more serious, but she still held a soft smile. "Mr. Patrick, I'm sorry for your father's poor health. But I really believe God can give him a complete recovery. He's God. He can do whatever he wants. Through the trial of your dad's stroke, God brought me to know your family, and I feel that I've been so blessed to know them. I just want to be a good doctor, and help any way that I can."

David tried to process what she had just said. Everyone around him was after a piece of the pie…immediate family and a few close friends being the only exceptions. Did she really want to help with no ulterior motive? No dreams of wealth and glamour? Even as untrusting as he had become over the last few years, he believed her. He really believed her. David looked at Sarah's smile and found himself wanting to touch those soft lips. Their gazes locked as he lost himself in the clear blue of her eyes, and Sarah felt her face flush. She quickly looked down at her hands, not wanting him to see into her heart. He slowly stood and eased toward the door, stuffing his hands into his pockets.

"I won't take any more of your time. I'm sure you've had a long day. But there is one thing I would like to ask. Would you please pray for Liz? She's not a believer."

Sarah felt like someone had punched her in the stomach. Her brow tensed. "What?"

David shook his head. "She's never accepted the fact that we're all born into sin, and Jesus Christ is the only way to heaven. I've talked to her, and so have Mom, Dad, John, Jennifer…and she listens, but her heart is hard. She uses hypocrites to excuse her own disbelief. She thinks that if she lives a good life, God will simply let her into heaven. I wish you would reconsider coming to help trim the tree tonight. We'd love to have you come, and it would really mean a lot to Liz."

She opened the door and led him down the hallway to the entrance door, thankful they were out of the close quarters of the examining room.

"Thanks, but I promised Jennifer that I would come and finish giving the children their yearly checkups. I'll call Liz and explain. In the meantime, I'll be praying that God will soften her heart to the gospel and that he will give me the right opportunity to talk to her. She will have to see his unconditional and boundless love and her own lost condition."

He took her small hand and covered it with his as he looked down into her eyes. Her heart quickened with his warm touch.

"She has a great deal of respect for you. When God opens the door for you to talk to Liz, I think she'll listen." He sighed and looked at the floor. "I pray that she will."

"I'll be praying for her too, Mr. Patrick. Good night."

He stood studying her face for just a moment, still holding her hand.

He flashed his gorgeous smile. "Good night. And it's David."

She caught a chill as she closed and locked the front entrance door behind him. And even though she tried to convince herself it was from the cool night air, she knew it wasn't.

Chapter Eleven

When David arrived back home after his meeting with Sarah, Liz was in a great mood. He found her just like he had left her—sitting in the great room on her cell. She was smiling and laughing. David always enjoyed hearing her laugh. He plopped down in the big chair next to the fireplace and laid his head back to rest. He breathed a prayer of thanks for how well everything had gone with Sarah. Mary and Maria came in carrying large plastic totes full of ornaments. He had been so lost in his thoughts that he didn't even notice the large Christmas tree that filled the corner. The piano had been moved out in front of the tree, giving the warm and cozy feel of the season.

Liz clicked off her phone. "That was Sarah."

David snapped his head to attention at the sound of her name. He wondered if she had told Liz about their meeting. Sarah didn't seem like the type that disclosed personal information, even to close friends. And Liz confirmed his thoughts.

"She said she had been very busy this week. The flu was going around, and she was sorry she hadn't called me back."

Liz looked at her mother. "She wanted me to thank you for the invitation, but she just couldn't make it. She said maybe another time. I think she also had to go to the children's home to give vaccines or something."

Mary didn't look at Elizabeth as she was busy concentrating on placing a big, red glittering ornament in just the right spot on the tree.

"Well, I'm sorry she couldn't come too. I really like that girl."

Elizabeth walked over and picked up an ornament hanger and placed it in a big red ball to hand to her mother.

"Yeah, me too. I invited her over to go horseback riding tomorrow. She said that Dad was her last patient, and she would be free the rest of the day."

David had settled his head back into the chair. He seemed to be completely relaxed, but in reality, he was taking in every word.

"Hey, Dave! Want to come with us?"

David roused up as if he hadn't been following the conversation.

"Come with who, where?"

"With me and Sarah horseback riding tomorrow."

"What time?"

"Oh, probably around four o'clock."

Dave spoke as he lazily rested his head back into the chair. "I might...if I'm home by then."

His eyes were closed while he made a mental note to be home no later than 3:00 PM.

Elizabeth watched him as he rested next to the fireplace. He had not said much since coming home. Where had he been? Since she was the one who typed up his weekly itinerary, she knew his schedule well. He had not been at another team meeting. Maybe he went to see John. No, that wasn't it. She remembered Jennifer telling her that John was meeting with one of the mission board members this evening. It was really none of her business, but she couldn't help but notice the soft smile that came across his face as he sat with his eyes closed. She was sure that a team meeting or a workout in the weight room wouldn't evoke that kind of joy. Mary and Maria were still busy with the tree as she slipped over beside his chair. He didn't move and neither did the smile. He was totally in a world of his own. She finally kneeled down beside him and tickled his cheek with her finger. He jerked and looked at her. She was grinning from ear to ear.

"What are you so happy about tonight?"

David's mind had been wandering to Sarah. Every time he closed his eyes, he could see soft blond hair, deep blue eyes, and a gorgeous smile. Had his face telegraphed what he was thinking? If anyone could read his thoughts, it was Liz. Not good.

He gave her an annoying look, as if she had just wakened him from a doze. "What are you talking about?"

"You were laying there with a silly grin on your face. I just wondered if you wanted to share the joy?"

Was he really grinning? He had to keep cool. "I always enjoy tree trimming night."

Elizabeth stood up, swinging an ornament around her finger and giving him a look that told him she didn't believe a word. "Uh-huh."

David's mind scrambled to change the subject. "Where's Dad? I thought he might come down. He always loves putting up the tree."

Mary was still concentrating on her ornament placement as she spoke. "He came down long enough to see us put up the tree and string the lights, but he began to get pretty tired. Besides, he had a busy day with the physical therapist. We took him back upstairs just before you came in."

David slowly got up and stretched. "I think I'll turn in too."

Liz eyed him. "It's only ten o'clock."

Ignoring her comment, he kissed his mom and said good night to Maria. He patted her arm as he swept past her. "Night, Liz."

He noticed that she didn't return his good night bidding, which meant this conversation was far from over.

When he reached his room, he sat down on the bed to remove his shoes. He remembered Sarah's face when he told her he had stuck both feet in his mouth, and he couldn't help but grin again. When he looked up from untying the laces, Liz was propped against the doorframe with her hands clasped behind her back and a knowing grin on her face.

"I'm glad you're so happy."

He ignored her and walked into his bathroom and closed the door. She heard the water come on and the sound of teeth being vigorously brushed. He was avoiding her. The glances he was giving Sarah the night of the dinner party were definite looks of interest. How could he not like her friend? She was awesome! If there was one girl in the world she would give a "thumbs up" for her brother to date, it would be Sarah. Dave hadn't fooled her. He was interested.

He finally emerged from the bathroom in his pajama pants and a T-shirt. She was standing in the same place he left her.

He pulled back the covers and crawled in. "Are you still here?"

"I just wanted to tell you that I really hope you can come with me and Sarah tomorrow."

He punched his pillows and settled back, with his muscular arms behind his head. "Well, I might. If I can get some sleep."

She chuckled and started to leave. "I get the hint. Oh, by the way. There was something I wanted to tell you about Sarah that's pretty funny."

She had piqued his interest, but he had to seem disinterested for Liz's benefit.

"What?"

"When I first met her, she didn't know who you were." Liz was laughing now. "I couldn't believe it at first, but she really didn't. I think it embarrassed her, and I try not to laugh about it. It's just that her life has been so different from what we're used to. You know, living in another country and everything. Do you remember the dress she had on Friday night?" David pictured it in his mind. How could he forget? "She made it. In fact, she makes all her clothes. They didn't exactly have shopping malls in the jungle, so they made everything. She's been totally responsible her whole life and had very little opportunity to relax or enjoy anything. I'm trying to help her in that department. Sarah's been all work and no play for too long."

David talked with his eyes closed. "I don't know. I think I like her the way she is. In fact, it might help if she rubbed off on you instead of the other way around."

Elizabeth put a hand on her hip. "What's that supposed to mean?"

David chuckled. "It means that you still haven't typed up my itinerary for January."

"Oh, yeah? It's on your desk. But I wouldn't expect you to notice such things, with your head so far up in the clouds."

He looked at his sister with one eyebrow lifted. "Have you been watching daytime talk shows again?"

"Okay, go ahead and make fun. But this girl couldn't care less what your name is, *or* who you are. I just wanted to give you fair warning, dear brother. If she seems to know nothing about you, don't let your ego get too deflated."

He gave her a bland reply. "I'll try not to be too crushed."

Elizabeth breezed out of the doorway. She could read him too well, and he didn't know how much longer he could hide his interest in Sarah from Liz. He gave a long sigh of relief that she had moved on.

Suddenly, she reappeared in the doorway. "And don't think you're hiding anything. I know you like her."

Elizabeth's head met with the thud of a pillow and a stern, "Good night, Liz!"

Chapter Twelve

Sarah was not an experienced rider, so she was glad the terrain was not very difficult to maneuver. She held on tightly to the reins, hoping the horse would just follow David and Elizabeth's lead. It was hard not to notice how good David looked on the chestnut brown horse. In his jeans, button-up shirt, boots, and Stetson, he looked like a Western hero. But she wasn't going to let herself get distracted by this man. Oh no. She had responsibilities and must ignore the hard thump of her heart. He was her best friend's brother. Besides, he would never be interested in a simple missionary girl, who didn't even know what texting was until three days ago. Over the past few days, she had paid more attention to the television in the break room at work. Hardly a day went by that David's name wasn't mentioned on the local channels. Elizabeth was kind. She hadn't made fun of Sarah's lack of knowledge concerning David...or anything else for that matter. Elizabeth liked her just the way she was. That was true friendship. Sarah had been praying for the right moment to talk to Elizabeth about Jesus Christ, but timing was everything. God would have to prepare her for such an important conversation.

The horse trail on the Patrick property stretched far behind the main house, down to a clear, bubbling stream. Sarah dismounted and led her horse, Winnie, down for a drink. David watched as she rubbed the velvety nose and spoke gently. It was obvious that Winnie had taken to Sarah. But who wouldn't? His mind kept going back to the evening at her office. He remembered how much he had dreaded the encounter. She had somehow made what should have been a very uncomfortable meeting into a nice way to spend an evening. When he thought of her, he could only think of two words…beautiful and gentle. Usually, women made him uptight, but Sarah could put him completely at ease. Well, if you could disregard the pounding pulse and knot in his stomach every time he saw her. One thing was for sure. She wasn't a man chaser. He couldn't tell whether she had any interest in him or not. She was kind, but that was just Sarah. She was kind to everybody. This was new territory. She had made it more than clear that she wouldn't be easily swayed by external things, like fancy cars and big houses. And that was just one more reason to admire her.

They had gotten a late start, and the sun was beginning to set a breathtaking pink and gold. As they turned for home and the stables, he rode up beside her.

"You're doing very well. I thought you said you didn't know how to ride."

She gave him a shy grin. "I think Winnie's just a very good horse."

"She's really taken with you. I think you may have a friend for life."

Sarah smiled and patted Winnie's neck. "I sure hope so. She's beautiful."

Winnie gave a big nod, as if she approved of Sarah's assessment of her.

David's laugh rumbled a low baritone. "I believe she's agreeing with you."

Elizabeth was up ahead when her cell phone rang, and she grabbed it from her blue jean pocket. After a few moments, she turned back to David.

"There's a problem in scheduling your flight to Dallas next month. I need to get back to the house and make a few calls. Can you stable Rocky for me?"

"Sure. Go ahead."

Sarah watched Elizabeth nudge Rocky into a gallop and head toward the stable.

"She takes good care of you, doesn't she?" It was more a statement than a question.

"Liz is a good one. She started handling all my appointments and scheduling about a year and a half ago. I have to admit, she's good at it." He grinned. "If anyone could enjoy yakking on the phone for hours at a time, it's Liz."

Sarah laughed. "I'm still trying to get used to my pocket ringing every few minutes. Cell phones are a new concept for me. Most of the students had a cell phone when I was in medical school, but it was a luxury that I didn't think was necessary at the time. I never owned one until I came here, so I guess you could say I'm technologically challenged."

David flashed her one of his smiles. "That's not necessarily a bad thing. There are days when I wish I could throw my phone in the nearest lake. You don't know how blessed you are, to have lived most of your life without one. They call them modern conveniences, but they're more like modern headaches."

Sarah followed behind David's horse into the stable and watched him dismount.

"I'm enjoying this new life of mine, but I still have a lot to learn, and I admit that I miss the simplicity of my home in Honduras. I know it'll take me a while to adjust. You know, change." She began her slide down to the ground when she was suddenly caught around the waist by two muscular arms and turned toward him. His eyes locked to hers. "No. Don't ever change."

Heat rushed to her face as she stood in his arms for what seemed like an eternity. He was incredible. She was speechless, staring into those warm eyes that were studying her face.

He finally spoke softly. "I guess I need to unsaddle the horses." But he didn't move.

She cleared her throat and swallowed hard. "Sure."

He pulled himself from her to begin stabling Rocky. Sarah's mind was reeling. What should she do? Say? Did she see something in his eyes? Was he interested in her? Her? A nobody from a nowhere place? Maybe this was just the way of American men. Maybe he was simply trying to be helpful to his sister's friend. *Pull yourself together, Sarah, and offer some help. He was just being nice.*

"Can I help you? I'm not sure what to do, so you'll have to show me."

He was lifting the heavy saddle off of Rocky's back. "That's all right. I can manage. You can go back up to the house if you want. I'm sure Maria's got cookies baked by now. She always has some ready for us after we ride."

"That sounds nice. See you at the house." He didn't respond as she turned to walk up the path toward the patio entrance. Was it her fault that they lingered together in each other's arms too long? Should she have moved more quickly? He had caught her completely off guard. What was she supposed to do? She put a hand to her forehead and winced. All this emotion and boy-girl thing was just too foreign. She didn't want to be another "Elsie" or false friend, like Elizabeth had before. *Oh, Lord, teach me what to do. I'm so embarrassed and ashamed. I know I didn't handle that situation right.*

When she finally reached the door, Elizabeth was waiting, looking out the tall glass window of the great room beside the fireplace. She had to pull herself together.

Elizabeth gave her a confused look. "Where's Dave?"

Sarah looked over her shoulder toward the stable, still breathing hard. But it wasn't from the walk. "He's coming. He was taking the saddle off Rocky when I left. I offered to help, but he said he could do it, and for me to come enjoy some cookies." She was trying to stay calm and collected, but her hands were still trembling when she took a cookie from the plate that Liz held up in front of her.

Elizabeth studied her as she asked. "Want some milk?"

"No, thanks. I'll just take the cookies and be on my way. I've got a long day tomorrow. Tell Maria I said thanks, okay?"

Elizabeth watched her friend back very nervously out of the room as she talked. "I really enjoyed the ride. I appreciate the invitation. See ya, Liz!"

This wasn't the typical, always-in-control Sarah. Elizabeth smiled. Something had happened at the stable, and she had a sneaky feeling that a certain brother of hers had something to do with it. Getting him to spill the facts, now that was the challenge.

David finished stabling the horses for the night. It was nice to be alone with his thoughts for a few minutes. He grabbed a brush and started stroking Winnie. With every stroke, his heart ached. Holding Sarah for just a moment was more than he could put into words. He knew that he had caught her by surprise, and she seemed very flustered, but she didn't pull away from him either. When he looked into her eyes, there had been fear. Not the kind that was caused by a sense of physical danger, but rather a fear of the unknown. She was definitely not the kind of girl who played the field. He desperately wanted her to know that she could trust him. But how did he prove that? Hopefully, the more they got to know one another, her trust would be won. It had been an enjoyable day, and he found himself longing for many more in Sarah's company.

After brushing Winnie, he placed the brush back on the shelf and closed her in the stall. Winnie placed her velvety, white nose over the rail in the hope of getting a rub, and David obliged.

"Well, Winnie. I guess I'll just have to keep praying about this one. Good night, girl."

He secured the stable and began his walk up the path to the back door when he spotted Elizabeth peering out of the big glass window. She hadn't seen him yet. He dodged around some shrubs to make his escape up to his bedroom by way of the kitchen and service elevator.

Okay, he admitted it. He really liked Sarah. More than anyone he had ever known. It was tormenting him that he didn't know how she felt about him, but he was not about to let Liz know or he would never hear the end of it. He knew his sister wanted him to be interested in her best friend, but he didn't want to give her the satisfaction of a successful matchmaking. Call it sibling rivalry, but he would never let her in on the secret until he could win Sarah's heart on his own. He took off his Stetson and slid his fingers through his dark hair, ready for a good night's sleep. If that is, he could get a certain lady's face out of his mind long enough to catch a few Zs. When the elevator door opened, Elizabeth stood staring at him with arms crossed. Then her face broke into a broad smile.

"Good night, Dave."

She turned to walk down the hall to her room, and she felt the thump of a Stetson hat hit her on the backside—along with a bland, "Night."

Chapter Thirteen

The steaming hot veggie soup from her thermos smelled wonderful. Having lived in a tropical climate where the temperature rarely dipped below eighty-five degrees, hot soup had never been a family favorite. But the Denver weather had changed over the last couple of days, and there was a cold wind whistling around her office window. She could feel the soup go all the way down, and it seemed nice to relax for a few minutes. Her next patient wasn't due for another half hour. It had been another very busy day, but there was a good side to that. Her mind had stayed away from David.

Beep! "Dr. Phillips?"

"Yes, Millie?"

"There's someone here to see you. A Mrs. Jennifer Hawks."
"Oh! Send her in!"

Sarah glanced over at the big cardboard box of toys in the corner. The toy drive for the children's home had been a great success. She hadn't told Jennifer how many toys they had collected over the last two weeks but wanted it to be a surprise.

There was a soft knock at the door.

"Come in."

Jennifer peaked in. "I hope I'm not disturbing your lun…" She stopped mid-sentence when she spotted the huge box in the corner filled to the brim with toys. "Oh! Sarah! This is awesome!"

Sarah was all smiles. "I thought you'd be pleased. Would you like some soup?"

Jennifer walked over to the box and picked up a bright yellow dump truck. She was so excited that she didn't hear Sarah's offer of soup. "This is the most we've ever gotten. How on earth did you manage to collect so many toys in only two weeks?"

Sarah walked over to put her arms around Jennifer's shoulders as they both looked at the mountain of toys. "God is good."

Jennifer leaned her head to one side onto Sarah's. "Yes, he is."

The sound of a cough came from the door, and Jennifer whirled around. "Oh! I'm sorry. Where are my manners?" She walked over to the door. "Sarah Phillips, this is Tiffany Smith. She's just out of college and came by yesterday looking for a job. We needed the help, so we hired her on the spot."

Sarah extended her hand. "I'm pleased to meet you, Tiffany."

Tiffany never stopped chomping her chewing gum. "Yeah. Same here."

Sarah put her hand on her hips and chuckled as she looked back at the toy box. "How are we going to get all of this into your car?"

Jennifer smiled. "We always wrap the gifts at the Patrick's, so Dave is coming to pick them up with his truck." She looked at her watch. "He should be here any minute."

There was a knock on the doorframe, and the three ladies looked around to see David standing in the doorway with his hands in his jean pockets, smiling that killer smile. "Talking about me?"

Jennifer stepped over to give him a handshake. "Dave! Thank you so much for doing this! Look at all the toys Sarah collected. I can hardly believe it!"

Sarah was glad that Jennifer was there to make conversation since she couldn't think of a thing to say. When her name was mentioned, David looked at her...and kept looking. He finally noticed the toy box. "Wow! That is a lot. I think that's the most you've ever had, isn't it? I'm glad I brought Steve along to help."

Jennifer put a hand on Tiffany's arm. "I'd like to introduce you to our new employee, Tiffany Smith. She'll be helping us wrap gifts tonight too."

David nodded. "Nice to meet you."

Tiffany swayed over within inches of David's face. "I'm *very* glad to meet you."

Jennifer was so excited about the toy drive that she didn't notice Ms. Smith's obvious move toward David. She was like a kid in a candy store, and the excitement was contagious. "It'll take us half the night to wrap all of these. Oh! Sarah, I forgot to ask. Do you think you could come and help wrap gifts tonight? We sure could use the extra hands." David and Steve had already begun toting toys out the back entrance.

"Sure! I'd be glad to. What time?"

"Mmmm...about six?"

"Sounds great. I'm hoping to be free by four o'clock today."

"We'll have a great time. Bring your appetite with you. Mary always has quite a spread of refreshments for all of us busy elves."

Sarah laughed. She had rarely seen Jennifer so giddy. They finished taking the toys out to David's truck, and Sarah rushed back into the office to see her next patient and finish up her day. Christmastime sure was exciting around here! Wrapping presents by a real Christmas tree. What fun! The digital clock read one fifteen. Would four o'clock ever come?

When Sarah finally arrived at the Patrick home, everyone was gathered in the great room, distributing the gifts to be wrapped. The Christmas tree gleamed in the corner behind the baby grand piano, and the fire popped and crackled in the large stone fireplace. The smooth voice of Nat King Cole flowed softly from the stereo, singing "The Christmas Song."

Elizabeth wrapped her in a big hug. "I'm glad you came! I was beginning to wonder if you would make it."

Sarah gave a weary smile. "I was at the office longer than expected. Sorry I'm late."

John's voice boomed across the room. He was wearing a Santa hat and his finest Christmas smile, clearly excited about the great number of toys for the children. "You're right on time! We're just now beginning to distribute the toys for wrapping."

Elizabeth gave her an appraising look. "You can't wear that to wrap gifts in."

Sarah looked down at her business suit and heels. "Sorry. I didn't have time to change either."

Elizabeth grabbed her hand and pulled as she yelled back at the happy wrapping crew. "We'll be back in a few!" And she whizzed Sarah up the steps.

Fifteen minutes later, Sarah reappeared in a pair of Elizabeth's jeans, a pink Denver Wolves sweatshirt, and white fuzzy socks. She had pulled her hair up into a ponytail with a bushy mane. David looked up from his wrapping detail to smile at her new look. *Cute. Totally cute.*

Everyone had found a spot on the floor and surrounded themselves with toys, paper, scissors, and tape. Sarah found a spot between Jennifer and Tiffany and began to survey all the gift wrapping accessories. "I admit that gift wrapping is not exactly my area of expertise."

David overheard her comment and tried to think about what her life must have been like in such a poor country. Did they even get to enjoy Christmas presents? Something nudged his heart, and it wasn't sympathy. Sarah had proved that she could do anything she set her mind to with God's help. What he felt was an overwhelming wave of respect. He watched her as she picked up a toy, trying to assess the proper amount of paper needed. It was clear that she was trying her best to have a good attitude in spite of her shortcoming. After a few minutes of paper cutting, taping, tucking here and folding there, she had finished her task. With the mountain of gifts that had already piled in the middle of the floor, he couldn't see her finished project. Sarah just sat and stared as she bit her lower lip. She began to chuckle, and then it turned into full-blown laughter as she held up what had to be the most miserable-looking package ever.

"Tell the kid that gets this one that it got run over by a reindeer."

Everyone burst into laughter. Elizabeth looked at Jennifer. "If I ever need surgery, please don't let Sarah do it." That brought a new wave of laughter as Sarah threw an empty paper roll at her friend.

Three hours and fifty-two presents later, John placed the last gift in the big box. "Wow! That was a job! I don't know what we're going to do with all of these between now and Christmas."

Mary and Maria were bringing in trays of refreshments. David reached for a glass of punch. "What about my weight room? There's plenty of room in there."

John took a cup of hot cider and a cookie. "Are you sure? That's a lot of packages."

"No problem. They won't be in the way."

"I appreciate that, Dave."

David took a bite of a homemade cheese cracker. "Sure."

Sarah thought about how down-to-earth David was. Her impression of him had completely changed since their first meeting. She remembered thinking the words *"pompous jerk."* That seemed so ridiculous and even embarrassing now, and she was exceedingly grateful that she hadn't said those words to his face. It just goes to show that it takes time to really get to know people. And there are two sides to every story. She understood now why he reacted the way he did. He really was a nice guy. She wished him well. There were many wishes in her heart, but those were best left buried. It was better just to be content with the status quo. That way there would be no hurt or bitter disappointment down the road.

Everyone was enjoying the wonderful refreshments. Maria sat down a tray of sandwiches, and Sarah watched as Tiffany reached for one with her left hand. There was an obvious impression on her ring finger that sparked Sarah's curiosity. At their first meeting in the office, earlier that day, she had felt an odd uneasiness about Tiffany. Jennifer said that she was fresh out of college, but that didn't match the lines around her eyes and other age-telling features that perhaps only a doctor would notice. This woman was much older than early twenties. If she had to guess, she would say it was more like early to mid-thirties. Jennifer really seemed to like Tiffany, but something wasn't right.

After everyone had stuffed themselves with finger foods, John suggested a sing-a-long around the piano. He grabbed Jennifer's arm and pulled her toward the baby grand.

"No, John. I can't play a lick. Get Sarah to play the guitar again."

Sarah laughed. "Oh no. It's your turn to be in the hot seat."

John was persistent. "Come on, Jen. I know you can play a few Christmas songs. I'm not asking for the 'Hallelujah Chorus,' just 'Silent Night' or 'Away in a Manger.'"

Jennifer plopped down on the piano bench. "Oh, all right. But I'm expecting a great Christmas gift as a reward for this personal humiliation."

She began the introduction for "Away in a Manger," and everyone gathered around. They finished the first verse and chorus, and John brought them into the second verse. Sarah was enjoying the wonderful harmony that filled the room. She glanced around at all the happy faces. But there was a face missing. Tiffany's.

When the song was over, Sarah excused herself. "While you guys start 'Silent Night,' I'm going to check on Mr. Patrick. I'll see if he feels like joining us."

She made her way to the foyer and up the stairs, scanning every room as she went. It was possible that Tiffany simply went to the bathroom, but as she passed the guest bathroom on the main floor, the door was open and light turned off. The same was true for the small bathroom next to the kitchen entrance.

When she reached the top of the stairs, she noticed movement at the end of the hallway. Tiffany was carefully, and silently, coming out of one of the rooms. When she turned and saw that Sarah had spotted her, she looked surprised but recovered her expression. She walked easily down the hall toward the stairs.

"Hi, Sarah."

Sarah gave a bland, "Hi."

Tiffany was trying to be cheery and nonchalant. "I had to go to the little girl's room. I hope I haven't missed the sing-a-long."

"No. They're still singing."

"Great!"

Sarah watched as Tiffany quickly bounded down the stairs, and something churned within her. Tiffany had lied. Why would she pass two bathrooms on the main floor to come upstairs and use the second-floor restroom? She was after something. But what? And how could she prove it? *Help, Lord.*

She peaked in to see Mr. Patrick resting soundly. He had been with the physical therapist all day and progressed very well, so she decided to let him rest.

When Sarah returned to the great room, John, Jennifer and Tiffany had already left. Mary and Elizabeth were helping with the clean-up, while David was carrying the last of the packages to be stored in the weight room.

She moved out of Mary and Maria's way as they carried trays of left-over cookies to the kitchen.

"Can I help?"

Elizabeth handed her a dirty paper plate and cup. "Well, if you insist."

Sarah grinned. "Sure. Where's the trash can?"

"Over there. Next to the door. When it's full, Maria will take it out."

Sarah walked over to dump the plate and cup. "Did Jennifer survive all of John's Christmas song requests?"

Elizabeth laughed. "Up until 'The Twelve Days of Christmas.' She gave up at 'five golden rings.'"

"I'm glad your mom invited them. They needed a break."

"Yeah. They seemed to enjoy themselves. And I liked Tiffany too. I'm glad they brought her along. I invited her and Jennifer over for lunch tomorrow. Think you could come?"

"Thanks, but I've got a full schedule tomorrow. I'll call if anything changes, though."

"I hope you can make it. Tiffany was interested in the horses too. We might do a little riding while they're here."

Sarah made no comment about Tiffany as she placed the last bit of crumpled wrapping paper in the trash. "Well, that's the last of the mess in here. Is there anything else I can help you with?"

"No, that's everything. Thanks for the help."

"No problem. It's getting late, so I guess I should head home." She reached to give Elizabeth a hug. "I had a great time. Thanks for the invitation."

"You bet. Drive safely."

"Thanks. Talk to you later," She headed for the door. "And tell your mom I said thanks!"

"I will. If you can make lunch, we're meeting at eleven thirty."

"Okay. Night."

"Good night!"

Chapter Fourteen

Sarah sat in her office, studying the chart of one of her patients. But she simply couldn't focus. She reached into her purse and pulled out the little piece of paper with the license plate number scribbled on it. Something was nudging her to find out all she could about Tiffany Smith. When she and Jennifer had come to the office to pick up the toys, they were driving Tiffany's car. A blue, four-door sedan. And as they were leaving, she had made a mental note of the license plate. Maybe she was just being silly about it. Tiffany Smith was probably harmless. She looked at the clock. Eight forty-five. If she was going to accept Elizabeth's lunch invitation, she would need to give her a call soon.

Sarah walked out of her office and up to the reception area for a cup of Millie's good coffee.

"Morning, Millie."

Millie swung around in her chair. "Morning, Dr. Phillips."

Sarah began pouring a cup as Millie rose from her chair and made her way over to the coffee counter. She lowered her voice.

"I'm sorry to hear about David Patrick. How is the family handling the scandal?"

Sarah nearly dropped her cup. "What? What scandal? What are you talking about?"

Millie leaned closer. "You know. The one about him and a certain woman."

Sarah just stared.

"Oh, come on Dr. Phillips. It's all over the news. Don't you ever turn on a television?" Sarah could feel the heat rising up her neck, and her face getting hot. "I don't know what you're talking about, Millie. But I do know the Patrick family very well, and I can assure you that David Patrick is an honorable man. He would not do such a thing."

Millie walked back to her chair. "Whatever you say. But there's a reward for anyone who can prove it."

Sarah looked at Millie in disbelief. "A reward? That's pathetic. Some people will do anything for a dollar."

She whirled around and strode back toward her office when she suddenly stopped. Her mind was putting it all together. The scandal, the reward, and Tiffany. It all fit.

She closed her office door and quickly picked up the phone.

When Sarah arrived at the Patricks' for lunch, Jennifer, Tiffany, and Elizabeth were already seated at the little bistro table, sipping their iced tea.

She hopped up into her chair. "Hi, guys! Sorry I'm late. It's been a busy morning as usual."

Elizabeth laughed. "And I'm used to you being late…as usual."

Sarah gave her a wry grin. "Ha. Ha. Very funny."

Jennifer picked up a bowl of salad. "Have some Caesar salad. It's great!"

Sarah dished some into her bowl and Maria came with a steaming baked potato. "Wow! This looks wonderful and I'm starving."

Elizabeth stuck a fork into her already-half-eaten potato. "Then dig in. You're behind."

Sarah took a bite and looked over at Tiffany. "How are you enjoying your new job at the children's home?"

Tiffany was eyeing her with uncertainty. "It's fine."

Jennifer chimed in. "Oh, she's been wonderful! She mostly helps with the laundry. For the first time in weeks, I've actually seen the bottom of the laundry basket."

Tiffany gave a faint smile. "Yeah. Doing laundry is lots of fun."

Sarah laughed. "So how do you like the children? They are such sweethearts."

"I don't really care for children."

Sarah raised her eyebrows. "You work at a home for children and you don't like kids?"

Tiffany shot her a drop-dead look. "I needed a job, okay?"

Jennifer tried to ease the tension. "I hear ya. Jobs are hard to come by these days. If you can find one, you'd better grab it."

After the main course, they all enjoyed a small bowl of orange sorbet. Elizabeth ate the last bite of her dessert and swiped her mouth with a napkin. "Tiffany, are you still interested in horseback riding today?"

"Uh...sure."

Jennifer pushed her plate away. "I'm ready when you are. How about you, Sarah? Will you have time to stay?"

"I'd love to, but I have to get back to the office. I do have a few minutes, though. I'll walk down to the stables with you and visit Winnie. I brought an apple for her."

Liz chuckled. "You're spoiling that horse."

"Hey. Any horse that'll walk softly and not toss me into the nearest bush gets an apple from me."

They rose from the table and headed out the side entrance when Tiffany stopped at the door. "I just remembered. I need to make a phone call first. You guys go ahead. I'll catch up."

Jennifer stepped outside. "All right. Just follow the path. It'll take you to the stables."

Tiffany watched as Elizabeth, Jennifer, and Sarah made their way down the stone path toward the horses. When they were out of sight, she tiptoed quietly up the back stairway to the second floor. She listened at the door for just a moment before opening it and stepped into the hallway. All was clear. This was going to be easy. All she needed was anything with DNA. A toothbrush, hairbrush, tissue…practically anything from a bathroom medicine cabinet. She had located David's room the night before. Now it was just a matter of getting what she needed and getting out as quickly as possible. The hundred thousand dollar reward was practically in her pocket.

She eased open the bedroom door. All clear. The bathroom was just a few steps away. She stepped in the doorway when the light suddenly flipped on.

"Howdy there, little lady."

Tiffany gasped and whirled around. Steve stepped out from behind the door.

"Or should I say, Mrs. Kendal?"

Stephanie Kendal was busted, and she knew it. There would be no wiggling out of this one. But it was worth a try. "Stephanie? I don't know what you're talking about, mister. My name is Tiffany. Tiffany Smith."

Steve crossed his arms. "Oh, I don't think that's right at all. My background check says that your name is Stephanie Kendal, and that you work for a local newspaper as an investigative journalist."

Stephanie stared with fire in her eyes and her jaw clinched. "So, what now?"

Steve sighed. "Well, I've just been standin' here in the dark, waitin' for you to show up, so I could give you this little piece of paper. Since you're a journalist, I imagine you like to read."

He held up a paper in front of her, but her eyes never left him. "What is it?"

"It's a little thing that we lawmen call a restraining order."

She sneered. "There's nothing you can do. Freedom of the press, you know."

"In that case, I'd like to add a little footnote of my own."

Virtuous

Steve got nose to nose. "If I catch you within a hundred yards of the Patrick family, their friends, or their property, you're gonna find out just how rough and tough a Texan can be."

On her way back to work, Sarah was anxious to hear from Steve. Finally, her cell phone rang, and she reached inside her purse to retrieve it.

"Hello. Steve?"

"Hi, Doc. You were right…about everything. Her real name is Stephanie Kendal, and she's an investigative reporter. She and another journalist friend of hers concocted the whole scheme. One made the accusation and sold the story to national media. And when a big-time magazine offered a reward for any proof, Stephanie got on the inside to gather DNA that could be planted as incriminating evidence. Then they could collect the reward and also be promoted as journalistic heroes for a job well done. Another good guy taken down by the media."

Sarah could feel her stomach churning. How could anyone be so set on destroying an innocent person?

"Oh, Steve. I'm so glad you caught them before it got that far."

"Hang on now, I don't think I can take any credit for this. If you hadn't caught on to Mrs. Kendal, she might've been successful in destroying Dave's reputation. I know he and his family will be more than grateful."

Sarah pulled into her parking space and turned off the engine. "Wait a minute, Steve. I don't want David, his family, or especially Jennifer knowing about this."

"But, Doc…"

"It would crush Jennifer if she knew that she was in any way responsible for bringing someone to the Patrick home that was intent on ruining their reputation. And Elizabeth is very protective of Dave. She would feel awful about inviting that woman to lunch today. When Tiffany came out to the stables after you had confronted her, she gave the excuse of a headache so that she could leave inconspicuously. Liz and Jennifer didn't suspect anything amiss. Please, Steve. Promise me that you won't tell them what *really* happened, unless you feel that it's absolutely necessary."

Steve blew out a sigh. "All right, Doc. If that's the way you want it."

"That's the way I want it. Thanks, Steve."

"Bye, Doc."

"Bye."

Chapter Fifteen

A couple of days had passed since Steve had caught up to Stephanie Kendal, and already, the media hype had begun to die down. Sarah had noticed a definite sense of relief in the Patrick household. No one ever mentioned anything to her about it, which meant that Steve had kept his promise.

When Sarah sat down in her office to swallow a quick bite of lunch, she checked her voicemail. *Beep!* "Hey, Doc! It's Liz. How's it goin'? I just wanted to see if you'd like to come with us to a Christmas concert tonight. Yeah, I know Christmas is over. But the Denver Symphony always gives an encore performance the week after Christmas. We go to it every year to beat the post-holiday blues. It's really great! We'll be leaving around six o'clock. Give me a call. See ya!" *Beep!*

Sarah clicked off her phone. The symphony? That sounded nice, since she had never heard one live. Her mom used to have an old record of the London Symphony Orchestra, and she remembered listening to it over and over. Heavenly music. That's what it was. The thought of getting to hear it in person was exciting. But the thought of being with David was, well, terrifying. Why couldn't she get him out of her mind? Her emotions were getting way off course. And why? Because he had helped her down from her horse. Big deal. He was just being nice. She had scolded herself a thousand times for even giving it a second thought. Okay, so he's a Christian, thoughtful, respectful, successful, and incredibly handsome. That's no reason to get all moony over this guy, right? Right. Besides, he would never be interested in her. She was the wallflower of the world. Public attention was never one of her ambitions in life. And where men were concerned, she was not willing to compromise her character by acting like a pompous airhead to get *anyone's* attention. She had seen enough of American gals to figure that much out. If that's what guys around here were looking for, then she considered being overlooked a compliment. God would bring the right person into her life when the time was right. Of that she was absolutely certain. But that still didn't solve her David problems. She was not of his world of newspaper and television cameras. He would be more interested in someone glamorous, which definitely ruled her out. She was totally happy with her new friendships…Mary, Elizabeth, Dr. and Mrs. Barlow, John and Jennifer. Everything was going well with Mr. Patrick's physical and speech therapy. So, she should be really happy, right? But there was an empty place. Something nagging at her very soul. She was determined not to let this thing with Elizabeth's brother get her off track. He was just a nice guy, and she would consider him a friend. But the symphony? What should she wear? She would have to hint around to Millie for some details and ideas.

David had decided to hit the gym early, and it had nothing to do with avoiding Liz. At least that's what he told himself. If he was going to make it to the symphony tonight, he needed an early start. Besides, a little weightlifting might help clear his mind. Fat chance. He was definitely "in like" with one Dr. Sarah Phillips and was looking forward to seeing her again...whenever that would be. After a morning workout, a press conference, and an afternoon with the pitching coach, he was exhausted. But the Christmas concert was a family tradition, and his dad had agreed to go, which made his mom very happy. They had reserved box seats. He had given Steve the night off, so he planned to slip in just after the concert began to avoid any publicity. He pulled into a parking place, stepped out of his truck, and hit the lock button on his keyless entry. It was just a little past seven and the concert had begun. He could hear the strings playing the opening piece of "Sleigh Ride," one of his favorites. Making his way up the staircase and through the corridor, he located the door to the box seats. He reached for the door when he noticed the knob turning. Someone was coming out. He backed up into the soft light of the corridor to make room, hoping there wasn't a problem with his dad. The door opened quietly and carefully as Sarah slipped out into the quiet space, her back to him. She slowly closed the door, trying not to distract from the music and turned around.

She gasped as she bumped into a very dashing David Patrick. He was quite an image, standing tall in his tux. After schooling herself all day to get a hold of her emotions, the sight of him sent her pulse into overdrive and her heart raced. He put his hands on her arms and smiled.

He softened his deep voice. "We can't keep meeting like this. Are you all right?"

She was breathless and he was too close. Waaaay too close. *Keep it together, Sarah.* "Y-Yes, I'm fine. I'm sorry I bumped into you like that."

He looked down at her. She was amazing, in a creamy white, long-sleeved gown with patterns of pearls swirling down the length. The high collar in the back gave way to a sweetheart neckline in front. Her hair was pulled up into an attractive style, with sprigs of golden curls falling down the sides of her face. Beautiful. He stared at her for a moment, and his chest tightened.

"Can I help you with something?"

She looked down and then over to the side, desperately trying not to look into those warm, brown eyes.

"I got a page, so I was just stepping out to make a call."

He gently rubbed his hands up and down her arms. "I hope everything's all right."

What was a girl to do? She finally looked up at him for just a moment then quickly back down.

"Yes. I hope so too." She started to move to the side and he moved with her, still standing just inches away. His aftershave lotion was dreamy, and she mentally scolded herself for even thinking it. He slid his hands down to hers, holding them firmly, but tenderly.

Leaning in close, he whispered, "By the way, you look beautiful."

The heat rose to her cheeks as he flashed a dimpled grin and stepped past her to get to his seat.

He was gone, but Sarah's hand was still trembling as she tried to dial the numbers. What *were* the numbers anyway? She rolled her eyes at herself and pulled the pager back out of her handbag. This was dreadful. Why did she act like this around him? She would simply have to keep her distance until she could get this emotional problem of hers under control—however long that would take. The page turned out to be something minor, so she wouldn't have to cut out in the middle of the concert. When she opened the door leading back to her seat, she noticed there had been a change in the arrangements. Elizabeth had moved up a row with her parents. And the only seat for her was directly behind them, beside David. Was she happy about that or terrified? She gave him a glancing smile as she took her seat. *Just concentrate on the concert.*

Sarah's spirit soared with the music. Listening to it on the phonograph had been nice, but hearing it live was just…well…heavenly. It wasn't just the sound. It was everything. The garland and bows streaming along the balcony and the huge Christmas tree standing tall behind the orchestra members, who were all dressed in black dresses and tuxedos. The concert ended with "Handel's Messiah," much to the delight of the audience. Thundering applause filled the hall, followed by a standing ovation, as the conductor took a bow and gave a wave with his long arm to the skilled musicians behind him.

As the applause began to fade, people began streaming out of the building, making a low hum of conversation and commenting on the music as they headed for the exits. The Patrick's all took a seat to wait for the building to clear.

Elizabeth turned around to Sarah. "So, what did you think?"

"I've never heard anything so beautiful in my life. It was amazing."

Mary turned and gave her hand a warm squeeze. "We're glad you could come. Maria was busy making a coconut cake when we left. Can you come enjoy a piece with us?"

"That sound's great, but I have a busy morning. Can I take a rain check?"

"Sure, dear. We'll save you a piece for when you come tomorrow evening."

Sarah smiled. "Thanks. I'll look forward to it."

David was paying close attention to the conversation between the ladies and felt a nudge of disappointment when Sarah refused his mother's offer for cake. He wanted more time with her. A lot more.

Elizabeth stood up and looked around the building. "Looks like we're all clear."

David helped Sarah with her coat and pulled on his long, black overcoat while Elizabeth rolled Jack out in his chair followed by Mary.

David touched his mom's arm. "Sarah and I will take the stairs. We'll meet you down at the elevator on the main floor."

Before Sarah could think, he had his hand low on her back guiding her to the staircase. When they reached the first step, David took her hand and her mind raced. *He's just being a gentleman. The staircase is long and steep.*

"So, have you ever been to a live concert before?"

She smiled a weak smile, trying to forget that her hand was warmly tucked in his. Being with him just felt right, even though she knew it shouldn't. He would never be interested in her. Not really. But was it a crime to enjoy this little bit of attention? It would undoubtedly be a fleeting moment.

"No. This was my first."

"They do a spring concert as well. It's good too." He laced his fingers in hers, sending her heart into fast forward. "Would you like that?"

"Oh. I'm s-sure I would."

When they reached the main floor, Sarah heard her name.

"Dr. Phillips?"

Sarah turned around to spot Carol Barlow, with a big smile spread across her plump little face, headed toward her with arms wide open for a hug. "Why, I didn't know you were going to be here. My sister and I always come to the encore performance. It's our winter tradition. I would like for you to meet her, but she stepped over to speak to a friend that she spotted in the crowd." Carol was eyeing the magazine cover man standing behind Sarah, so Sarah began the introductions.

"Mrs. Carol Barlow, this is a friend of mine, Mr. David Patrick. I work with Carol's husband, Tom."

David held out his huge hand to take hers. "I'm pleased to meet you, ma'am."

She took his hand and her little round face scrunched up into a big smile. "It's nice to meet you, young man. I'm sure you know what a fine, young lady you're out with tonight. I don't know what in the world we would do without her. Everyone loves Sarah!"

David looked at her with an amused grin. "I couldn't agree more."

Sarah could feel her face flush. Mrs. Carol obviously didn't know any more about the sports world than she did and didn't recognize David or his name. What's worse, she made it seem as if they were together, and that couldn't be farther from the truth. She had to save herself this embarrassment. She scrambled to correct the assumption that had been made about her and David. Not that she objected to the idea, but she knew that was not how he saw things.

"Mr. Patrick's father is one of my patients. I was invited to join the family tonight." *Now it's time to change the subject.* "Wasn't the concert beautiful?"

Mrs. Carol took the bait. "Oh my, yes! I think this is the best they've ever done. But I say that every year."

David was a little disappointed at how quickly Sarah had corrected Mrs. Barlow's mistake about them being together. But then, she would never be presumptuous. It was simply her character, and he admired her greatly for it.

David's cell phone rang, and the ladies' conversation became a low hum in his ear, as he pulled the device from his pocket to read the illuminated screen. It was Elizabeth.

"Excuse me." He stepped away and leaned against the wall to have his conversation.

Elizabeth sounded impatient. "Where are you two?"

"Sarah ran into a friend. They're talking right now." He looked over at her as she stood with Mrs. Barlow. The long gown captured her lovely sense of style, and he found himself captivated by her warm smile as she tilted her head slightly to one side to listen to Mrs. Barlow. She was the essence of grace and beauty.

"Oh. We'll wait."

David seized the opportunity. "That's all right. You guys go ahead. I can take her home."

If you can hear a smile, David could hear Elizabeth's, loud and clear across the connection. "That's very gallant of you. Gee, what a nice guy."

"Bye, Liz." Click.

Sarah ended her conversation with Mrs. Barlow. She looked around for David and finally spotted him leaning against the wall. He was watching...correction...staring at her. There was something in that look that was thrilling. When she spotted him, he straightened his broad shoulders and began his athletic stride toward her. He was tucking his phone back into his coat pocket but never took his eyes off her. Her heart skipped a beat, and her stomach tied itself in a thousand knots.

"Sorry about that. I hope she didn't think I was rude."

Sarah let her eyes follow Mrs. Barlow as she exited the building. She couldn't look at the man at her side. "Oh no, I'm sure she didn't." She turned to look down the back hallway. "Well, I guess we should go. I'm sure your family is wondering where we are."

He cleared his throat. "Uh...it's all right. They've already left. I told them I would take you home."

Sarah looked up at him, her eyes wide. "Oh. I'm sorry. I know you must be tired. It's been a long day and now you have to drive me home. I shouldn't have talked so long to Mrs. Barlow. I can call a cab."

He took her hand again and gave her a look that melted her heart. "It's no problem. Didn't you hear? I'm lucky to be out with such a fine lady."

Sarah's shoulders slumped. She put a hand to her forehead and closed her eyes. "I'm sorry about that too. I'm so embarrassed."

He gently brushed a wisp of blond hair that had fallen into her eyes. "Don't be embarrassed. I wholeheartedly agree with Mrs. Barlow." Sarah blushed. It had been so long since David had seen anyone blush over anything that he had to smile. Sarah gave him a desperate look. "Poor Carol. She didn't know who you were. She didn't know that I'm just an employee of your family. I hope you're not upset."

David's smile faded and he looked deep into her eyes. "No. You're not just an employee, Sarah. You're much more than that."

Sarah swallowed hard, not wanting to read more into his words than she should. Her heart fluttered again, and she tamped it down. "I didn't mean to sound cold. Your family has never treated me like an employee but rather like a friend. You'll never know how much that's meant to me."

David studied her face as she spoke, wanting to draw closer until there was nothing between them. He was falling. And falling hard.

Chapter Sixteen

The air was frigid, and a cold wind began to blow as David guided Sarah to his forest green four-wheel drive truck. He clicked the unlock on his remote and stepped around to let her in the passenger seat then rushed around to slide behind the wheel. Sarah was so cold her teeth were chattering. David clicked on the heat. "It'll be warm in a minute."

"F-fine. I'm still adjusting to this climate. Is it always this cold?"

He rubbed his hands together and blew into them before shifting into *Drive*. "No. Most of the time it's colder."

Sarah chuckled. "I never had any reason to knit a sweater while in Honduras, but I think I had better learn. And fast."

David glanced over at her. He could smell her soft, flowery perfume. "Did you make all of your clothes while you were there?"

"Yes, and I still do. Well, everything except for a few items that Elizabeth helped me pick out the other day."

His brows knitted together in disbelief. "Do you mean that you *made* that dress?"

She looked down and began smoothing imaginary wrinkles from her lap. "I made this last month for the Medical Convention Banquet. At the time, I thought it was such a waste since I didn't figure that I would ever wear it anywhere else. But tonight was a good excuse to pull it out again."

Okay. David's respect level just hit a new high. Every time he thought she couldn't be any more remarkable, she surprised him again. Most girls would have maxed out a credit card just to try and impress him. But this lady didn't feel a need to impress anyone, including him. Which was…well…very impressive. And the more he thought about it, the more he agreed with Carol Barlow. *He* was the lucky one.

She guided him through the city streets out to a little rural area apartment. He noticed they were in close proximity to the children's home. No doubt, she had chosen this particular apartment complex with that in mind. It was nothing fancy but very well kept. He pulled into her parking space and put the truck into "Park."

He took her hand as she slid out of the passenger seat and walked her up to the door.

Sarah began digging in her handbag until she finally pulled out her key. She was wrestling with the idea of asking him to come inside. Would that be appropriate or not? So, all she could think to say was, "It's freezing out here."

David's back was to her as he stood with his hands in his coat pockets and looked toward the bright light that illuminated the parking lot. "And it looks like we're in for a bit of snow."

Sarah whirled around and practically pushed him aside. "Snow?!"

"Yeah. The weather forecast said there was a 90 percent chance tonight." He watched the flakes fall through the beam of light and into the darkness. After a moment, he realized that Sarah had fallen silent. She wasn't making a sound or a single movement. There was barely enough illumination from the street light for him to witness a tear trickling down her cheek. What was wrong? Was it something he had said? Did bad weather trouble her in some way?

He touched her arm. "Are you all right? Is something wrong? It's just a little snow. No big deal."

She stared at the flakes that were now as big as goose feathers. "It is, if you've never seen it before."

The snow was floating to the ground and slowly covering the truck windshield. David looked at her as she tilted her face toward the heavens with an expression of complete awe and wonder. "My sister Rebekah has always wanted to see snow." She let out a shaky breath. "Do you ever feel guilty because you are so blessed?" Another tear fell. "Someday soon, my sister will get her wish of snow. I'll see to it."

As Sarah stood in wonder of the loveliness that God had created, David stood in wonder of her. He had never met anyone so genuine. Someone who would let tears fall out of sheer thankfulness to God for something as simple as snow. Standing in her long white gown, covered by her winter coat, she took his breath away. He put his hands on her arms and turned her toward him. Their gazes locked, and he brushed away a tear with the back of his hand. His finger gently stroked the outline of her lips and he tilted her face toward his. His kiss was warm and tender as he caught her face in his hands. Sarah's heart raced and her breathing ceased as she felt the tenderness in his touch, and the gentle rhythm of his lips against hers. She opened her eyes to see him gazing into her own.

His voice was as soft and tender as his kiss. "Good night, Sarah." And she watched him disappear into the white night.

Chapter Seventeen

Sarah stood at her door and watched as David's truck slowly vanished from sight. Had he really kissed her, or did she imagine it? Her quick heartbeat and rapid pulse told her that it had been very real. She was afraid to move, hoping time would stand still. He had actually kissed her! But why? It had been so difficult to keep her heart in check around a man like David, and she had been determined to be sensible about the matter. She liked him. Really liked him. But her practical mind had refused to think that he might be interested in her. After all, he was a man of wealth and a celebrity, who could have anyone he wanted. So why in the world would he choose someone like her? The answer was simple. He wouldn't. *Okay, Sarah. Pull yourself together. This is America. It's probably just customary for a man to kiss a woman after he gives her a ride home.* Part of her wanted to argue with her practical reasoning, but she simply couldn't allow it. It would only lead to heartbreak. And being hundreds of miles from her family was hard enough without also having to deal with a broken heart.

Her mind whirled as her ear caught a faint ringing from inside the apartment. The telephone. She frantically twisted the doorknob, realizing that she hadn't unlocked the door yet. Scrambling for her keys, she pulled them out and twisted them into the lock. As she picked up the receiver, she noticed her hand still trembling.

"Hello?"

"Sarah? Is it really you?"

"Rebekah?!" Sarah sank down into the chair beside the phone table. "Oh, it's so good to hear your voice!"

Sweet Rebekah. If anyone could calm her nerves, it was her sister. She wanted to laugh and cry at the same time.

"It's good to hear your voice too. How's everything in *your* hemisphere?"

Sarah smiled. "Just fine. How about yours?"

"Pretty good. Busy. But good. I've been helping Bianca for the last few weeks. You should see Antonio. He's the spitting image of Bianca, but he has Jose's energy. That little guy is never still!"

"Well, give him a big hug and a kiss from me." Sarah laughed. "The baby that is, not Jose." It was wonderful to hear her sister's laugh. "How is everyone doing?"

"Well, Dad is staying busy making his rounds. Mrs. Cabrera is expecting another baby. Mr. Cortez is recovering from pneumonia. Oh, and little Pedro Ocho fell out of a tree and broke his nose. Mom has been cooking meals for several of the elderly. Tim, Joe, and Luke have been busy getting the spring tent meeting organized. What about you? Are you getting settled into your new job?"

"Yeah, it's going fine." Sarah tried to sound convincing, but she had heard the insincerity in her own voice and knew that her sister wouldn't buy it.

Rebekah's tone turned somber. "You don't sound fine. Are you sure?"

Who was she kidding? She wasn't fine. And hiding that fact from Rebekah would be nearly impossible. Although she was a world away, the tie that bound them as sisters was just as strong as ever. Rebekah had never betrayed her trust, and they had always been able to confide and pray for one another. And if she had ever needed prayer, it was right now. Still, the words just wouldn't come out.

"I'm sure. It's just the strain of the day."

"I confess that I'm worried about you. You've been on my mind all day, and I just felt like I should call. I hope you don't mind having a nagging little sister."

"Of course not. And no, you've never nagged." Sarah took a deep breath. "I could use your prayers, Rebekah. There's something in my life right now that I'm a little confused about, and I don't quite know how to handle it. I also would like for you to pray for my friend, Elizabeth. She's not a believer and I want to talk to her, but I also want the timing to be right and for God to give me the right words."

The line went silent for just a moment. Then, Rebekah's soft voice flowed across the miles as a wave of peace washed over Sarah's heart. "Heavenly Father, I come before you now on behalf of my dear sister. I pray for your peace to comfort her. You know and understand the matter that has caused her to feel confused and burdened. I also pray for Elizabeth, that she would see and understand what you did for her on the cross. Lord, I pray that you would give Sarah wisdom, courage, and love to handle these situations. I take great comfort in knowing that even though I'm so very far away from her, you are always near. In Jesus's holy name I pray, amen."

"I love you, Sarah, and I'll be praying for you every day."

In spite of her iron will to hold back the tears, her voice broke. "I...l-love you too, Rebekah. Thank you s-so much. Give Mom and Dad a kiss for me."

"Take care and I'll talk to you again soon."

"Okay."

"Bye."

"Good-bye."

Sarah placed the receiver back onto the phone and sat in the dark hallway wiping the tears that freely fell. Why was she so emotional? This wasn't like her at all. She had always been so steady and in control of herself. Between the excitement of the concert, her burden for Elizabeth, the wonder of snow, David's kiss, and Rebekah's phone call, it was as though the whole evening had been the roller coaster ride of a lifetime. Maybe she was just tired. Her nerves were frazzled. She bolted the door lock into place, turned off the light, and headed for the bathroom. Over the years, she had found very few things in life that a long hot bath wouldn't cure.

The windshield wipers were on "high" now, and visibility was minimal at best. A dusting of white snow was quickly covering the roadway as David's pickup slowly maneuvered down the two-lane highway. He knew that he needed to concentrate on the slick road conditions, but it was hard to focus. He wanted to think about the woman he had just left and the way his lips still remembered her warm touch. He wanted to think about her silky hair, her sweet fragrance, and her soft voice. But just as his mind wanted to wander, his tires would hit a slick spot and bring him back to the here-and-now.

The drive back home should have taken about twenty minutes. It had taken an hour. He pulled into the garage and turned off the engine. After the door rolled down, closing him into the darkness, he slumped down into his truck seat and closed his eyes. His chest was tight as he thought of her. He lifted his hand to rub his forehead and caught the scent of her fragrance that was still on his hand. *Oh, man. I've got it bad.*

God, you know I love her. Please show me how to win her heart.

The warmth inside the truck was quickly being replaced by frosty winter air. He stepped out into the darkness of the garage and headed for the side door. Snow had already covered the walkway leading to the back entrance, and big flakes continued to fall as he flipped the collar up on his coat to protect his neck and ears from the cold. Halfway up the walk, he stopped. Elizabeth. She would, no doubt, be waiting with that knowing look and triumphant smile. Hmmm…she wouldn't expect him to come in through the front door. He stuffed his hands in his coat pockets, jogged back down the walk and turned the corner to the front of the house. He reached the steps and took them two at a time. His hot breath was a cloud of white in the cold night air, as he dug into his pants pocket for the right key. He turned toward the porch light, fumbling for the right one.

"Looking for something?"

Elizabeth.

He swung around to see her leaning against the doorpost with her arms crossed and a definite, knowing look and triumphant smile. Well, the only thing he could do now was try to blow her off.

"Just looking for my key. Thanks for waiting up. This weather's getting worse by the minute. Night, Liz."

He tried to breeze past her, but his chest was met with a boney, little finger.

"Did you take Sarah home?"

He backed up, still standing outside. It was obvious that Liz was going to let him enjoy the cold until she got her questions answered.

"Uh... yeah. I got her home okay. It didn't start snowing until we got to her apartment."

With hands in his pockets, he was bouncing to avoid the chill. "Move, Liz. I'm freezing." He really wasn't that cold, but it was a good ploy to end the conversation.

Her smile widened, and before turning to go in the house, she leaned forward to give him a soft tap on the nose with her finger. "You kissed her, didn't you?"

She sashayed into the foyer, when suddenly, a big snowball smacked her right in the back of the head. She whirled around. "Hey!"

David had already darted past her and made his escape up the stairs. But he could hear Liz's laughter behind him as she called after him. "I was right!"

Chapter Eighteen

The next morning, Sarah awoke to a rumbling sound outside her apartment window. She slipped on her robe and tiptoed across the cold, hardwood floor to lift one slat of the blind and peer out the window. The plow had just begun to clear the snow-covered parking lot. When the good Lord sent snow to Denver, he really meant business. There was at least a foot of the white stuff. Her car was buried and would have to be dug out. She looked at her nightstand clock. Five forty-five. There wouldn't be any time for coffee this morning, if she had any hope of digging out and getting to work on time. The thought of driving was nerve racking. She had never even seen snow—much less driven on it. Her memories of the muddy Honduran pig paths didn't seem so bad now. Her bottom lip pooched out to blow an unruly stray hair out of her eyes. Well, no use procrastinating. She clicked off the alarm on her clock and headed for the bath.

After buttoning up the big winter coat and pulling on boots and gloves, she was ready to face the daunting task of uncovering her car. But with what? Until that moment, it hadn't occurred to her that she didn't even own a shovel because up until now she had never needed one. Now what? She stood at the door and looked around the apartment to assess what would be useful in just such a predicament. Ah! A broom would probably work. She pulled her broom from the kitchen closet and headed for the door when the doorbell rang. Six thirty. She mumbled to herself as she crossed the room to look out the window. *Who in the world would be here at six thirty in the morning?* Maybe it was a neighbor who needed help digging their own car out of the snow. She peeped out the front window curtain to see a green truck in the space next to her car, and her pulse raced. *He wouldn't come at six thirty in the morning, unless it was an emergency.*

She quickly opened the door to see a very cold but handsome David in a big brown winter coat and gloves with melting snowflakes in his black, tousled hair. He was carrying a box of pastry, with two cups of coffee perched on top and wearing a dimpled grin to die for.

One side of his mouth rose into a half smile and his baritone rumbled. "Morning."

Her heart skipped a beat. No. Make that two beats. "Morning."

"I thought you could use a ride to work. Not that I doubt your driving skills. But I didn't figure you were used to driving in the snow."

She stood, with tongue tied and brain frozen.

His smile widened. "Mind if I come in? It's a little cold out here."

Pull yourself together, Sarah. "Oh! Yes, of course. Please come in."

She pulled back the door and stepped out of the way as the smell of coffee, pastry, and masculine aftershave moved past her and into the foyer.

"You can set it on the counter. I'll get some plates and napkins."

He pulled off his coat and situated his large frame on a stool at the counter to begin opening the box of pastry. She could feel his gaze on her as she took a couple of dessert plates and napkins from the kitchen cupboard. "Wow! That smells great!"

"I hope you like cherry."

She slid onto the stool beside him. "I love cherry. Thanks. You must be a very early riser to have made it here by six thirty."

"Not really. I just couldn't seem to sleep much last night."

She knew why he hadn't slept because she had experienced the same restlessness.

He turned to her, and their gazes locked with a knowing look. He smiled. "Want me to ask the blessing?"

All she could do was nod. He took her hand in his and bowed his head. "Lord, thank you for what we are about to receive. I pray that you would keep us safe and make us a blessing to all those that we encounter today. In Jesus's name. Amen."

As she lifted her head, he laced his fingers in hers. "I hope you don't mind me coming without calling first." His brow tensed. "Maybe I should have called."

He was so large, sitting close beside her. He was all she could see, and the view was quite nice. It was hard to ignore the muscular frame that was more than evident through his long-sleeved T-shirt.

She gently squeezed his hand and gave him a soft smile as her face grew warm. "No. I'm glad you came."

Unsure of what she could see in his eyes, she quickly looked down and released his hand to take a bite of the delicious cherry-filled delight. But all she could taste was the kiss from the night before.

He could feel her uneasiness and decided to lighten the subject. "So, what do you think of Colorado snow?"

Sarah's tense shoulders eased and she smiled. "It's great! How much snow did we get?"

"Oh, I'd say about a foot and a half."

"Wow! That's a lot. Is that a usual amount?"

David took a sip of the steaming coffee. "Maybe a little more than usual. But get used to it. I'm sure there'll be more before the winter is over. You'll probably be sick of it by spring."

"Never. I could never be tired of snow." Sarah polished off her plate and took a final sip of her coffee. "This was great! Where did you get it?"

David swiped his mouth with his napkin and placed it on his empty plate. "I got up about five o'clock and began baking."

Sarah laughed. He loved her soft, bubbly laugh. "No, really."

He chuckled. "The wife of one of my teammates has a bakery near here. It's called Cake and All Things Yummy."

Sarah stacked his plate on top of hers and headed for the sink. "I'll have to check it out some time."

"Yeah. Sabrina's a great gal. She opened her first bakery in North Carolina and just recently opened one here in Denver. Her husband, Jonathan, smuggles cookies in to our practices all the time. Needless to say, he's the most popular guy on the team."

Sarah smiled. "I can certainly see why. Dr. Barlow's wife, Carol, is having a birthday at the end of the month, and he'll need a cake. I'll mention Sabrina's bakery to him." David rose from his chair and walked into the kitchen. "I'm sure she'll appreciate the good word."

She ran warm water into the sink and poured a couple drops of dish liquid in to begin washing. "So, when do your practices start?"

David picked up a towel. His arm brushed hers as he took the first plate and began polishing it.

"In about three weeks. I have to be in Talking Stick on February 2."

"Talking Stick? Is that really a place?" Why did the thought of him leaving give her heart a tug?

He rumbled a low laugh. "It's in Arizona near Phoenix. That's where we have our spring training."

"How long will you be there?"

He polished off the last plate. "About six weeks."

Sarah pulled the drain plug and watched the water swirl down the drain, along with her mood. "Oh."

David walked over to the coat rack and pulled back on his big winter coat. "Well, if I'm going to get you to work on time, I guess we had better start moving."

Sarah tapped down the feeling of loneliness that had engulfed her heart and went to retrieve her coat, gloves, umbrella, and bag of extra clothes that she had packed in case of an emergency.

The ride to the office had her captivated. The trees looked as though someone had piped white icing over the tops of each branch, and the roadway was marked with slushy, black, tire tracks. Several cars had slid out into the side ditches, and a rumbling snowplow spewed dirty, black snow into a long heap. David's face was tense, and he said very little as he slowly maneuvered through the slick roadways. He finally relaxed as they pulled into the office's back parking lot. "Can I help you get inside?"

She reached for her bag and umbrella. "Oh no. I can manage. You've done enough already. After watching you drive on this stuff, I don't think I would have wanted to do it. Thank you so much."

He reached over and covered her hand. "You're welcome. What time do you get off?"

It hadn't occurred to her that he would have to take her home too. "Uh...about five."

He flashed his dimpled smile. "I'll see you then. Have a good day."

She gave him a shy look. "You too."

After opening the door, she popped open her umbrella and stepped out into the snow to head for the door. She could feel him watching her as he waited in his truck for her to get safely inside. What was she going to do about this? His attention was something she had not seen coming. How could she diligently keep her heart when Mr. Wonderful kept showing up and doing thoughtful things? This was definitely not the image she had of professional athletes. But with David, it was hard to remember that he was a pro baseball player. She felt totally at ease with him, if you could disregard the heart pounding every time he came within a hundred feet.

Sarah reached her office and sank down into her chair to take a deep breath. This was ridiculous. There was no way that he was romantically interested in her. He was probably just being nice for Elizabeth's sake. It was obvious how much he loved his family, and he had told her what a hard time Elizabeth had finding friends. So that had to be it. At least that was what she would tell herself, and she was going to stick to that story—or she was in for a big-time heartbreak.

It had been another busy day, but that was nothing new. Lunch had been nothing more than a granola bar and a quick sip of milk, and she was definitely feeling the emptiness in her stomach. Four thirty. David would be arriving at the back door soon. She stepped into the private, half-bath to comb through her hair, convincing herself that it was perfectly normal to tidy up after a long day of work. It had absolutely nothing to do with a certain someone, who was coming to pick her up soon. As she pulled off her lab coat and slipped back into the big overcoat, David's truck appeared outside her office window. Part of her almost wished he would've forgotten to pick her up so that the thousands of butterflies swirling in her stomach would land. It seemed so strange to be totally comfortable with someone and yet so nervous at the same time. The truck door opened, and a large boot stepped out into the slush as an enormous black umbrella popped open. She had been so busy that she hadn't even noticed that it was snowing again. He was coming to the door to get her. There it was again. Thoughtfulness. Why did he have to be so nice? If he could be just a little bit arrogant or obnoxious, it sure would make her life a lot easier.

Chapter Nineteen

Sarah turned out the light in her office and reached the door, just as David was coming up the steps. As the big glass door swung open, a gust of icy wind nearly knocked her over, and she turned her face away, until suddenly she felt sheltered from the blast of cold. It had been replaced by warmth and the scent of woodsy aftershave. When she turned back around and pushed her hair back, she met the warm gaze of soft brown eyes.

"Are you all right? That was quite a gust of wind."

"Yes. I'm fine. Thanks."

He stood just inches from her face, unmovable. "I'm a little bit early. Are you ready to go?"

She could feel the heat moving up her neck to her face. "Y-yes. I've already locked up."

He wrapped his arm around her and held the gigantic umbrella with the other, as he guided her down the slippery, snow-covered steps and through the parking lot to his truck. When he helped her into the passenger seat and started around to the driver's side, her senses picked up the wonderful smell of Chinese food. Her stomach made a rumble, reminding her of the skipped lunch.

David swung into the seat behind the wheel, cranked the engine, and fired up the heater.

"Did you have a good day?"

"Very busy. How about you?"

"Same. After my workout, I went to help John and Jennifer assemble the new bunk beds for the kids. You should have seen them. They were so excited."

Sarah smiled. "Who? John and Jennifer or the kids?"

David smiled. "Both. I didn't figure you would be very busy today with the weather being so bad. Didn't you have any cancellations?"

"Nope. Not a one. It was just as hectic as usual."

David glanced over at her when they stopped for a traffic light. "In that case, I'm glad I brought dinner. I hope you don't mind. I thought it might help, after a long day of keeping Denver well."

Sarah laughed. "I don't think I'm doing such a great job of keeping Denver well. In fact, I think all of Denver is sick, and I saw them *all* today. As for dinner, I could eat a bear."

"Sorry, but it's chicken."

She smiled over at him and shrugged a shoulder. "Well, I guess that will have to do."

As soon as they arrived at Sarah's apartment, she turned on the gas logs and dashed to her room to change clothes. That morning, David hadn't really taken much notice of her apartment. But now that he had a moment to look around, he took note of how orderly and tastefully decorated it was. Nothing fancy, just nice and cozy. The neutral colors of cream and brown, with hunter green and burgundy accents, made it warm and inviting. The mantle over the fireplace was decorated with various picture frames, and the coffee table in front of the plush sofa boasted a large album with a picture of Sarah and presumably, her family. The corner was occupied by a huge bookcase filled with books, candles, and more photos. It was easy to see how much Sarah's family meant to her.

Sarah reappeared from the bedroom, wearing jeans, a gray sweatshirt, and sneakers. David couldn't help but smile. Cute.

"Make yourself at home. You can put your coat over on the rack, next to the door."

He hadn't realized that he was still wearing his big overcoat. "I was just looking at all of your pictures."

Sarah began removing the boxes of rice and chicken from the big paper bag while David took his coat over to the coat rack. "The photos on the mantle are of my family, and the ones on the bookshelf are mostly of my friends in Honduras. After we eat, I'll show them to you. Do you like iced tea?"

"Uh, yeah. Sounds good."

She sat the two glasses on the dining table. David's on one side and hers on the other, along with two steaming plates of rice, veggies, and sweet and sour chicken. It hadn't escaped her attention that the little candle in the center of the table had been lit while she was gone to change clothes. He pulled out her chair, and then she watched him reach over to slide his food and drink to the spot beside her. After lowering himself into the chair, he took her hand and bowed his head.

"Lord, thank you for this food and for bringing us here safely. Amen."

The meal was either exceptionally delicious or she was exceptionally hungry. But either way, it was very hard to swallow with David so close. During the dinner conversation, she tried to focus on her plate since looking at him seemed much too intimate, given his close proximity. And she certainly hadn't forgotten the kiss from the night before.

After dinner was over and the dirty dishes lay soaking in the warm, soapy water, she joined him in the living room as he stood in front of the fire, observing the mantle again. She stood beside him, still drying her hands on the dish towel. He was looking at the various photos. She pointed to a wooden frame that bordered a very muscular young man in his mid-twenties, wearing dark sunglasses, with arms crossed, leaning against a black jeep, and looking very formidable.

"That's my brother, Luke. We call him the protector of the family. He has a tough-guy exterior, but he's really a big marshmallow." She chuckled. "I would never tell him that to his face, though. That picture was taken at my grandparents' home in Texas. That old jeep is Papa's pride and joy."

The next frame matched the first one, but this guy was wearing camo pants and a brown T-shirt while holding up a snake and grinning ear-to-ear.

"This is Micah. He's the explorer of the family, as you can see." Sarah glanced over with a wry grin. "He knows how I hate snakes and gave me this picture as a going-away present. He thought it was hilarious."

She took down the next picture from the mantle. "This is Tim. He's Mr. Responsibility and completely predictable." Sarah smiled down at the photo. "He's also very dependable and big-hearted. He's a lot like my dad."

The next frame was different from the others. It was white, with hand-painted pink roses on its border. The young lady in the picture was hugging Sarah, and although their features were different, the smile was the same...soft and easy.

"This is my sister and best friend, Rebekah." David looked out the corner of his eye as Sarah got quiet. The long sigh that followed sent the message loud and clear. She missed her sister, terribly.

Deciding that it was best to move on, he stepped over to the big bookcase and looked at the large brass frame on the middle shelf. "Are these your parents?"

Pulled from her thoughts, Sarah joined him next to the shelf to view the couple standing with their arms around one another, smiling at the camera. David could definitely see the resemblance between Sarah and her mother. She took down the frame and softly wiped the glass with the sleeve of her sweatshirt.

"Yes. These are my parents, Mike and Katherine Phillips." She sat the picture back on the shelf and began introducing all of her other friends in the photos.

Sarah headed toward the kitchen to finish the dishes and left David leafing through the album on the coffee table. The thick book was her missionary life history. Everything from preteen years to present day was represented in the form of photos, letters, thank-you notes, and personal journal entries. Each time he flipped a page, he was more amazed. There were scores of people from all walks of life that had benefited from her compassion and medical expertise.

He was almost to the end of the album when she sat down on the sofa beside him. "That book was my going away gift from Rebekah. I never realized how much of our life she had captured on film through the years." She chuckled. "I knew I should have never gotten her that camera for Christmas when we were kids."

The last page was an eight by ten photo of Sarah and an interesting looking creature with its long hairy arms wrapped around her neck.

David cocked one eyebrow. "What is that?"

Sarah laughed. "That's Meeko, my sloth."

"Sloth?"

"They're native to Central and South America. My father and I took a trip to Peru to help out a fellow missionary, and I found Meeko in the jungle. He had been wounded, but he eventually made a full recovery, and I talked Dad into letting me bring him back home with us."

"What exactly does a sloth do?"

"Absolutely nothing. You know how the Bible talks about being slothful? Meaning lazy? Well, this little guy is where that term came from. Sloths do nothing but lie around, and they are very slow movers. Not such a good thing for people, but it works out great if you're a sloth. Meeko is the sweetest pet ever. Micah goes for the creepy crawlies. I go for the soft and cuddly."

She leaned closer to get a better look, and David inhaled her vanilla and sugary scent.

"I wish I could have brought him with me, but he would have never survived the Denver climate. So, I left him in Rebekah's capable hands."

David closed the book and placed it back on the coffee table. "You've led an eventful life."

Sarah cocked her head to one side and looked thoughtful. "Eventful." She chuckled. "That's one way of putting it. But then, so have you."

"Yeah, I stay busy."

"You don't sound very happy about that."

He leaned his elbows on his knees. "I enjoy what I do, but I don't really enjoy all the travel. I'm more of a homebody."

Sarah raised her eyebrows. "You? I never would have guessed it."

"I enjoy peaceful places. And thanks to my parents, I've always enjoyed a godly and peaceful home."

"Yes. I know what you mean. I always knew that I was blessed to have Christian parents, but I understand now more than ever, how much I took it for granted. I guess that's why I love working in the orphanage so much. John and Jennifer have given those children a loving and peaceful home, and it's a blessing to be a small part of that."

He looked into her lovely, deep blue eyes and found himself wanting a repeat of the night before. There was an amazing connection between them, that he knew only God could give…an inexplicable drawing of his soul to hers. But suddenly she looked away, as if she knew his thoughts, and her face blushed. She closed the book and placed it back on the table. "Would you like something else to drink?"

David knew he had overstayed his welcome. He didn't want to do anything that would compromise his testimony or hers, so he stood to his feet. "No, thanks. I need to get home. You've had a long day, and it's getting late."

He walked to the coat rack and pulled on his heavy coat. Sarah followed with arms crossed. "Thanks again for everything. The ride to work, dinner…everything."

He threw his scarf around his neck and then put his hand on her arm. "You're welcome. I'll see ya."

She closed the door behind him and peered out the front window as the truck headlights backed out of the parking space and pulled onto the main road. He was gone. The room seemed terribly large and empty. Why did she suddenly feel so alone? Why did her chest hurt? Why was she wondering when she would see him again? He had not tried to kiss her good night again, so maybe last night was just a "caught up in the moment" kind of thing…or an "American guy thing," as she had thought before. He considered her a friend of the family, and that was all.

Sarah took a deep breath, turned off all the lights, made sure the doors were secure, and headed for a long hot bath. Her grandmother had told her there was nothing that a good hot bath wouldn't cure. But her grandmother had never met David.

David walked into Elizabeth's office, and she whirled around in her chair. "Where have you been? Out with *Dr.* Phillips?"

"She's not used to snow. I drove her home from work."

"I'm sure she was appreciative." Elizabeth leaned back into her chair and crossed her arms. "It's funny. I've barely had a chance to talk to her in over a week. I didn't even get a chance to talk to her at the concert. She's always too busy. But she doesn't seem too busy for you."

David picked up his itinerary for March and glanced over it. "What's that supposed to mean? All I did was give her a ride home. Believe it or not, some people really are busy, Liz. It's winter. Doctors are generally busy in the winter. You know. Colds, strep throat, the flu…"

She twirled her pen between her fingers. "I've just been sitting here thinking. You see, I called Tiffany to invite her over for brunch tomorrow morning, and I was surprised at what she had to say."

David kept looking at his itinerary. "Uh-huh."

"Tiffany said that she was sorry to decline my invitation, but Sarah told her not to come around here anymore. Tiffany also said that she had to quit her job at the children's home because Sarah helps with the children every evening, and Tiffany is uncomfortable around her."

David looked up with a confused look. "That doesn't make any sense. Sarah would never make anybody uncomfortable."

Elizabeth gave him a cold stare. "She would if she was after you. It's happened before, you know. It all makes sense. She uses me to get to you, and then she gets rid of any competition."

"Liz, she's your best friend. I can't believe you're saying this. She's never given you any reason to doubt her loyalty."

Elizabeth's expression was hard as she stood to face him. "They all say they're a Christian. They're really just big liars. I'll never trust another so-called Christian again as long as I live." She balled her fist in his face. "So help me, Dave, if you ever mention God or the Bible around me again, I'll slug you."

David was stunned and speechless. He heard a voice behind him. "You're wrong, Liz."

Elizabeth glanced over David's shoulder to see Steve, standing in the doorway. "This is none of your business, Steve."

Steve walked over to Elizabeth, took her by the arm, and forced her back down into her office chair. "I've got something to say about this, and you're both gonna listen. Sarah made me promise not to say anything unless it was absolutely necessary, and I guess stopping a family fight would fall into that category."

David's brow tensed. "What are you talking about?"

"Do you remember the scandal that came out in the news a few weeks ago?"

Liz rolled her eyes. "Uh...yeah, Steve. I don't think any of us have forgotten that. But what's that got to do with Sarah?"

"Plenty. Do you also remember how it all went away? Almost overnight?"

David gave a slow, "Yeah."

Steve pushed his cowboy hat back on his forehead. "Well, you can thank Sarah for that."

Liz crossed her arms and gave a sarcastic "How so?"

Steve propped one hip up on the desk. "Well, Tiffany Smith is not Tiffany Smith. She's Mrs. Stephanie Kendal, an investigative journalist."

David put his hands on his hips. "What?"

"Yep. Sarah knew that she wasn't telling the truth about her age. She also caught her coming out of your bedroom when she went up to check on your dad the night of the toy wrapping party. Sarah was able to get a license plate number, and I did a background check. Turns out Mrs. Kendal, along with another reporter, were planning to sink your reputation for good. She was trying to get into the house so she could steal incriminating evidence to plant somewhere else."

David put a hand to his head. "Why didn't Sarah say anything about this?"

Steve looked down at a very quiet Elizabeth. "Elizabeth had invited Mrs. Kendal to the house for lunch. Sarah knows how protective Elizabeth is of you, and she didn't want to upset her *best friend* by telling her that she had invited danger into your home. She also thought of Jennifer. Mrs. Kendal used Jennifer to get into the house as well. She got that job at the children's home, knowing that John and Jennifer were good friends with your family."

Liz rose from her chair and started out of the room. David could see the tears streaming down her face. He gently touched her arm. "Liz."

She pulled away. "Not now, Dave."

Steve stood and crossed over the room to David. "I'm sorry for Liz. But she needed to know."

David gave him a soft slap on the arm. "She'll be all right. Thanks for everything, Steve." He started out of the room then turned back. "How did you catch her?"

Steve grinned. "That was Sarah's idea too. We set her up. When Sarah caught her coming out of your room, she was immediately suspicious. And when Mrs. Kendal kept her job at the children's home, we knew that she had not been successful in getting what she was after. She was waiting on another opportunity to get into the house. So, when Liz invited Jennifer and Mrs. Kendal over for lunch, Sarah knew that she would try again. But this time, I was waiting for her in your bathroom. I showed her a restraining order. It probably wouldn't stand up in court, but I think she got the idea." Steve chuckled. "You should have seen her face. She was completely shocked. It was beautiful. I haven't had that much fun since I was in Texas."

David grinned and started out of the room when Steve stopped him. "By the way, don't mention this to the doc. I promised her I wouldn't tell you unless it was necessary. And even though I felt that it *was* necessary, I don't want her to be upset with me. She's a peach."

David nodded. "Don't worry."

Chapter Twenty

David knocked at Elizabeth's door. "Liz?"
"Go away, Dave."
"C'mon, Liz. Open up."
"I said to go away."
"Can't we talk for a minute?"
"No."
David blew out a sigh and headed for his room.

Elizabeth tried to stop crying but the sobs kept coming, and somehow, that made her feel better. She deserved to cry. She had made a terrible mistake. Sarah was the best friend she had ever had. And what did she do? Accuse her of lying and manipulation.

She sat up, perched on the edge of the bed, and reached for a tissue. She would have to tell Sarah what she had done. The dread of that conversation was overwhelming. It would surely mean the end of their friendship. But it had to be done. And the sooner, the better.

Sarah looked at the clock. Ten fifteen. *Who in the world would be visiting this late at night?* She peered out the window. Liz. Something must be wrong. She opened the door to find Liz on her doorstep, shivering, and with a tense look on her face.

"Can I come in?"

Sarah swung open the door. "Of course! Get in here before you freeze to death."

Elizabeth stepped inside and stood for a moment, staring at the floor. Sarah could feel the tension. "Is everything alright? What's wrong, Liz?"

She kept staring at the floor. "I'm sorry to have bothered you so late."

Sarah closed and bolted the door. "It's no bother at all. But it *is* unusual for you to visit this late at night."

"I needed to talk to you."

"Here, let me take your coat." Sarah placed the heavy winter coat on the rack and waved Elizabeth toward the sofa. "Make yourself at home. Can I get you some coffee or something?"

Liz shook her head and took a deep breath. "There's something…I-I…need to tell you." The tears began to fall. "I've done a terrible thing."

Sarah's heart dropped as her imagination took over. What could have brought Elizabeth to such sorrow? She sat down on the sofa and placed a gentle hand on her arm. "Just take your time."

Liz let out a long, trembling sigh and gathered her composure. "You've been a wonderful friend to me and…I've l-let you down. You see, I talked to Tiffany today. She told me some bad things about you, and I believed them. I actually thought that you were using me to get to Dave and that you were trying to get rid of Tiffany because she was flirting with him."

Sarah's expression never changed. "Do you know now, that it isn't true?"

"Y-yes."

"So, what changed your mind?"

"Steve. He told me and Dave everything about *Mrs. Stephanie Kendal*."

Sarah looked down. "I see."

"Oh, Sarah! I'm so sorry that I doubted your friendship. You have a right to be upset."

Sarah smiled her soft smile and gently shook her head. "I'm not upset, Liz. You've spent a lifetime trying to protect your family. Over the years, you've become very cautious." Sarah gave her a wry grin. "You were just a little too cautious this time."

Elizabeth looked down. "I know."

"Don't get me wrong. Caution is a good thing. It takes time to know who we can trust and who we can't, and even then, we can be disappointed." Sarah gave a deep sigh. "But there is One that you can always trust and depend on, Liz. Jesus Christ. He loves you and will never forsake you. You can trust him completely. He loves you so much, that he died on a cross for your sins and mine. He wants what is best for you and wants to guide your life. Can you imagine having a best friend who knows the past, present, and future? That's pretty awesome."

Liz stood. "Sarah, I'm sorry for hurting you. I hope we can still be friends."

Sarah gave her a hug, knowing that Liz wanted the conversation to end. "Of course, we're still friends. The best."

Sarah watched as Liz got into her car and backed out of the parking lot.

"Dear Lord, please help her. She's running from your love, but she knows she needs it."

Chapter Twenty-One

"Awww! C'mon, Ms. Sarah! Read another one! Pleeeease?" Sarah walked over to the little red and blue two-shelf bookcase to replace the book she had just finished and reached for another one. When she pulled out *Miss Fluffy the Rabbit*, they all clapped and cheered.

"Yaaaaaay!" She carefully stepped around the children and sat back down in the big, wooden rocking chair.

"I'll only read one more story, and then it's bedtime." Sarah was trying to assert her "I mean it" look. But it was a futile effort. She was a pushover for sweet little faces—and they knew it. Of all the things she did at the children's home, story time was her favorite. It was such a joy to make a book come to life. As the story began, the children, who were seated Indian-style on little carpet squares at her feet, began scooting up closer to make sure they didn't miss a single word.

With all the commotion from the children begging for another story, Sarah didn't notice that John and David had stepped in behind her to listen. The children spotted them as they slipped in the open door, but John put a finger to his lips to give them the "shhh" signal. The room was dim, with only a couple of lamps lighting where Sarah was reading, and the two men faded into the shadows as they listened.

David watched the faces of the children as Sarah got to the part where Miss Fluffy finds the doll house to live in. Every child was captivated as they crept closer and closer to Sarah's feet. She leaned in toward them and lowered her voice as she told about the house. One of the toddler boys climbed onto Sarah's lap, but she never missed a word as she cuddled him close. You could hear a pin drop. A couple of the little girls yawned as Sarah closed the book. She had their complete attention and continued to whisper as she gave instructions for bed.

"You have been very good listeners. Now, I want you to quietly tiptoe to your beds, and I will come and tuck you in."

The children quietly rose to their feet, and without a word spoken, they softly padded off to their beds. Tyler, who had been on Sarah's lap, had slumped into a very comfortable sleep, and she leaned back into the rocker until everything became still. Then, she eased to her feet and carried Tyler to his bed, pulling the covers up to his chin and placing a kiss on his forehead. Every child received the same well-placed kiss and an "I love you, good night" as Sarah went down the line of beds until she reached the door. There was a slight movement in the shadows, and she squinted to see David standing with his hands in his pockets, leaning against the wall.

"That was a good story. I don't believe I've ever heard that one," he whispered.

"It's one of their favorites. What are you doing here?"

David had been watching Sarah so intently that he hadn't noticed that John had left the room. Her lovely face was touched by the soft lamp light, and his brain refused to function.

"Uhhh...I came to drop off some...uhhhh..." He swallowed hard.

Sarah raised her eyebrows, waiting for the answer that he couldn't seem to come up with. He just stared at her, so she tried to help.

"Toys?"

"No."

"Food?"

"No. Uhhh...clothes! Yeah. Clothes."

A few of the children who were still awake began to giggle. Sarah couldn't help but smile. She had never seen him so nervous, and it was kind of cute. She took his arm and guided him out of the room into the hallway where they could talk more freely.

"That was nice of you. I'm sure John and Jennifer appreciated the donation."

He shrugged one shoulder with his hands still in his pockets again. "It's no big deal. I'm just glad to help."

"Your father seemed well when I stopped by your house this afternoon. I can't believe the progress he's made in such a short amount of time."

"Yeah, we're all grateful for his improvement."

David looked at the floor and ran a nervous hand across the back of his head. "Look, I...uh...was wondering if you...um...that is if you're interested...uh..." He heaved a deep sigh. "About a week before spring training begins, we have a party at the stadium in one of the VIP suites for all of the families as kind of a *going away* thing. It's tomorrow night, and I didn't know if you would be interested in coming or not. Mom, Dad, and Liz will be there. Do you think you could make it?"

Sarah was quiet for just a moment as she tried to decipher the invitation. Was this an invitation for a date? Or did he simply want her on hand, in case his father needed assistance? Well, she wasn't going to presume the former, so she would go with the latter.

"I would be glad to assist your family. Mr. Patrick has been going out-of-doors more often, but his outings are still very limited. I believe he'll be fine, but I'll be on hand if he should need anything."

He looked confused for a moment. "That'll be great. Thanks. Well, I gotta go. I'll see you tomorrow night. Oh! It starts at seven o'clock."

She smiled. "I'll be there. By the way, is this formal or informal?"

He shrugged his shoulders as he backed away from her down the hall. "Mmmm...semiformal."

"Okay. See ya."

"See ya."

After saying good-bye to John, he went to get in his truck and headed home, totally frustrated as he mumbled to himself, "She must think I'm an idiot. I couldn't even remember why I was at the children's home."

Sarah desperately needed to leave the office by five o'clock in order to get home, change, and get to the party on time. But so far, nothing was going according to schedule. It was already four forty-five, and there were three patients still waiting. There was no way she was going to make it by seven o'clock, but maybe by seven thirty…if she was lucky and traffic wasn't too bad.

David anxiously looked at his watch and then over at the door. It was seven thirty and no Sarah. Jack sat in his wheelchair next to Mary, who was comfortably seated on one of the plush sofas while Elizabeth stood mingling with some of the wives. He took another long drink of his soda and noticed the door open as Sarah stepped into the room. His eyes never left her as she made her way over to Jack and Mary. One of his teammates walked up behind him. "Who is *that*?"

David cleared his throat and tried to give a nonchalant answer. "That's my dad's doctor."

"Wow! No wonder he's feeling better." He gave David a hearty slap on the shoulder. "Man, if that was my family doctor, I think I would find a way to come down with the flu, or something."

David took another sip of soda and made his way toward where Sarah was standing, talking to Liz. She looked amazing in a knee-length red dress. Her long, blond hair curled down her back as she stood with her hands clasped in front. He walked up behind her and rested his hand low on her back.

"Glad you could make it."

She turned toward him, looking apologetic. "Thanks. I'm sorry to be so late. I—"

He interrupted her as he took her hand. "Don't apologize. I'm just glad you're here."

He gently pulled her away from Liz. "C'mon. I'll introduce you around."

She stopped him. "You don't have to do that. I-I'm really not the social butterfly type. I'm perfectly happy being a wallflower."

He laced his fingers around hers and stepped closer, just inches from her face, as he lowered his voice. "Please. I want them to meet you."

She could see how much it meant to him. And she didn't want to seem rude toward his friends, even if it did make her a little nervous.

He introduced her to so many people, there was no way she would ever remember all their names. But each one was very open and friendly, which put her more at ease. David had not left her side all evening, and it seemed so nice. When he stepped over to speak with one of the coaches, she found a quiet spot where she could observe. Jack and Mary seemed perfectly content talking to other family members of players. Jack's clarity of speech had returned almost completely, and she was so happy for them both. This was such a precious family that God had brought into her life. She scanned the room until she spotted Steve sitting alone in a corner. Hmmm...another wallflower. Now that was more her speed. She liked Steve Travis. David had told her that he was a new Christian, and she knew what a good friend he had been to the Patrick family. He was respectful and every bit a gentleman, but it was as if there was something troubling him. Maybe he was just a loner and that was all there was to it. Well, she always found it easy to talk to Steve, and it looked like he could use some company, so she made her way across the room and sat down beside him.

"Hi, Steve."

He was leaning his elbows on his knees, drinking a soda. He responded but kept looking straight ahead. "Hey, Doc."

"Are you enjoying the party?"

He leaned back in his chair and glanced over at her. "Yes, ma'am."

Sarah smiled. "It's nice, but I confess I'm not much of a partygoer. Personally, I prefer a nice quiet evening at home. How about you?"

One side of his mouth curled into a crooked grin. "Yes, ma'am."

"David said that you used to be a Texas Ranger."

Sarah got yet another "Yes, ma'am," but she kept talking, hoping to somehow break his solemn mood.

"I was born in Texas. Lived there for eleven years until we moved to Central America. My dad used to be a Bronco Buster."

For the first time, there was a glimmer of life in those dark eyes as his eyebrows lifted in genuine interest. "Really?"

"Yeah. He and his buddies were always getting hurt, so he figured one of them should go into medicine...at least that's his story for becoming a doctor." She chuckled. "I loved Texas. What I remember of it, anyway. It's beautiful country."

Steve looked thoughtfully at the floor. "Yes, it is."

"Do you plan to return to Texas someday?"

"I've thought about it." He was quiet for a moment. "I guess you know that I had to tell Dave and Liz about Stephanie Kendal. You're not mad at me are ya, Doc?"

Sarah put a hand on his arm. "Not at all. I could never be mad at you, Steve. You're one of the good guys."

He grunted. "Thanks."

"David told me that you're a new Christian. I think that's wonderful."

"It took me a long time to make the decision...too long. My mom prayed for me for years, but I didn't make the decision till after she was gone."

Sarah looked at the floor. "Is that what's bothering you, Steve?"

One side of his mouth curled up. "Partly. My mom's birthday was yesterday. I've been thinking about her a lot."

"I don't know how it is in heaven exactly, but I do know the Bible says that the angels rejoice every time a sinner comes to repentance. So maybe your mom knows." Sarah smiled. "Maybe one of the angels told her."

Steve gave a faint smile. "Maybe."

"What about your dad?"

He looked down as he fidgeted with his soda can. "He's gone too."

"Sounds like you've had some tough years. Do you have any other family?"

"Grandparents and one sister. She's married with two kids. "

"And you never married?"

"No, ma'am." He leaned back in his chair and balanced on its back legs. "I'm a confirmed bachelor. If you don't get close to people, then when they die, it doesn't hurt as bad. Besides, I think I'm too old to consider a wife and family now."

Sarah's brows knitted. "How old are you?"

"Forty-one."

Sarah laughed. "That's hardly old, Steve. I think you're selling life short."

He lowered the chair back down to the floor and rested his elbows on his knees again. "Maybe. But I don't see any chance of my bachelor life changing any time soon."

"Have you prayed about it?"

"I'm new at this praying thing. It's always been hard for me to be open, even in prayer."

"There's not a secret formula to prayer. But I confess that it was a tool I often neglected in my Christian life until recent years, and it's been amazing how God has changed my life through prayer. It had always been my dream to come back to America, but I didn't think it was a possibility for me, so I never really prayed about it. Two years ago, my father preached a sermon on prayer. He talked about how we should be specific in our prayers. So, I began to pray that if it be God's will, He would send me to America. Eighteen months later, I received the letter from Bro. John requesting help in the children's home, and here I am." She put a hand on his arm. "Don't get me wrong, Steve. Sometimes, we pray for things that God, in his infinite wisdom, knows wouldn't be good for us. But there are other times when he just wants us to rely on him for the answers in our lives. God wants us to talk to him. As for you being too old or it being too late, I don't believe that for a minute. And I don't think you do either."

He took another sip of soda and looked at her. "You know, you're easier to talk to than most people. I bet you're a great doctor."

Sarah laughed. "Well, part of being a doctor is being a good listener. I've found that most people already know what the problem is, they just don't know how to solve it."

He lifted his can. "True" and took another sip. "What part of Texas did you live in before you moved?"

"Close to Waco. My grandparents still live there."

"Really? That's my old stomping ground. What are their names?"

"Bill and Anne Phillips. Do you know them?"

"Nope. Can't say that I do. But Texas is a big place."

"Well, if you ever decide to return to Texas, be sure and look them up. My grandmother is an excellent cook. They used to visit us once a year in Honduras. Grandmother makes the best apple pie you've ever put in your mouth. And do you like venison?

Steve started to answer when David came up beside them and took Sarah by the hand, as he pulled her to her feet and slipped his arm around her waist.

"What do you mean trying to steal my girl?"

Steve rose from his chair, ready to poke back at his friend. "Well, if she's your girl, I wouldn't recommend leaving her alone at parties."

David grinned. "I'll keep that in mind from now on."

Sarah looked back and forth in disbelief between the two men as they bantered over her. Did he say "his girl"? She felt excited and confused all at the same time. Was he just kidding with his friend? Should he be so presumptuous? He had never expressed any affection in words. She really liked David, but she didn't like to be trifled with. It was as though he had assumed a relationship without expressing it to her first. She enjoyed his attention but had no idea of his intentions and that left her with a great deal of uncertainty. How could she give her heart to someone who was not willing to be honest about his own feelings?

The cell phone in her handbag began to ring. "Excuse me." She stepped over into a quiet corner and looked at the illuminated screen. It was her brother Luke, which was very unusual. If Luke called, it was of the utmost importance. He was definitely a no-nonsense kind of guy.

"Hello?"

Luke's deep voice rumbled back. "Hi, sis."

"Hi! Luke. How are you?"

"Pretty good. I hope I haven't caught you at a bad time."

"No. Not at all. What's up?"

"I just wanted to let you know that Mom broke her foot and her wrist." Leave it to Luke to get right to the point.

"What?! How did that happen?"

"She was helping set up for the tent meeting, when she stepped in a hole. That's how she broke her foot. She broke her hand when she tried to catch herself from the fall."

"Oh, no! How bad was the break?"

"Dad says she'll be all right, but it'll be about six weeks before she heals. I know you're planning to come back next week to help with the tent meeting, but Dad wanted me to give you a heads-up on the situation. I think we've got everything covered for the meeting, but we may need you to look after Mom and take her place in the kitchen for the week."

Sarah knew how much her mom looked forward to the Tent Revival weeks. She always enjoyed cooking for all of the guests, but it was quite an undertaking.

"Sure. I'll be glad to help any way that I can. In fact, we have a new PA in the office, and I can probably work things out so that I can come home immediately.

She heard the relief in Luke's voice. Dad may be the doctor, but Mom made the wheels turn. "That would be great, sis. But if you can't work it out, we'll manage."

Sarah reassured him. "I'll work it out. I'll call you back to let you know for sure. Talk to you then."

"Okay. Talk to you then."

"Bye."

"Bye."

She ended the call as Liz walked over. "Are you all right? You look tense."

Sarah gave her friend a weak smile. "I'm all right."

Elizabeth could read the truth in her face. "No. You're not. What's wrong?"

Sarah wrapped her arms around her waist and heaved a long sigh. "My mom broke her foot and her wrist."

"That's terrible. I'm sorry to hear that."

"Yeah, me too. I'm going to check on your dad and then I need to go. I was planning to go back home next week, but I'm going to try and work it out so that I can leave in a couple of days instead."

"If you need to leave, go ahead. Dad's fine."

"Where is David? I wanted to thank him for the invitation."

"He's in another room talking to one of the pitching coaches. I'll tell him for you."

Sarah gave her friend a hug. "Thanks, Liz."

"You're welcome. I hope your mom will be all right."

Sarah smiled. "Thanks. God will take care of everything. I'm sure of that."

Liz watched Sarah slide into her coat and exit the room. She was the most honest and caring person she had ever met. Sarah was real. So why did she think she needed anything else to go to heaven? God certainly wouldn't send someone as nice as Sarah to hell. And he wouldn't send her either.

A few minutes later, David emerged from one of the side doors, scanning the room as he walked. Elizabeth tapped on his shoulder. "Lose something?"

"What?"

"I said, did you lose something?"

He never looked at Elizabeth as he continued to search the room. "No."

He started to walk away from her when she grabbed his arm. "She's gone."

He turned sharply. "Gone?"

Elizabeth's tone softened. "Come over here where it's a little quieter, and I'll tell you all about it."

After Liz gave him the details, he looked at his phone. Eleven thirty. It was too late to call her tonight. He would wait until tomorrow.

"By the way, have you told her how you feel yet?"

His brow tensed. "How I feel?"

"C'mon, Dave. It's obvious."

"To you maybe, but not to her."

"What do you mean?"

"I tried to ask her to come tonight as my date, but she just thought I wanted her to come and help take care of Dad."

"Did you tell her it was a date?"

"No. I didn't figure I had to."

Liz shook her head. "You've been around the wrong kind of women for too long."

"What are you talking about?"

"Dave, Sarah is not going to chase you. She's a lady. And she believes that it's the gentleman's place to make his intentions known. I know my friend pretty well, and I think she really likes you, but if you're waiting for her to throw herself at you, you're going to be waiting a looooong time."

Now David lowered his voice, but he was completely frustrated. "I gave her a ride to work and back home. I brought her breakfast and dinner. What more can I do?!" David caught himself before he admitted to Liz about the kiss.

Liz crossed her arms. "Tell her."

He froze. "Tell her?"

Liz gently patted his arm as she eased past him. "Tell her."

It was simple instruction, but it hit him right in the heart and shook him to the core. All his gestures of affection seemed easy compared to this. To even think of telling her how he felt made his stomach tie into a thousand knots. It would mean bringing down all the barriers and putting his heart on the line. It would mean no more games. Just the plain straightforward truth. And as bad as he hated to admit it, Liz was right.

Chapter Twenty-Two

David boarded the plane with his teammates. He shoved his duffel bag into the storage compartment overhead and slumped into the seat to stare out the window. Spring training had always been exciting, but at the moment, he felt absolutely miserable. After Sarah left the party Friday night, he had decided not to contact her until the next day since it was so late. He had a team meeting that morning and afternoon. By the time he called her late that evening, she was on her way to the airport. Now it would be six long weeks before he would see her again. And he really wanted to see her. It would have been six weeks either way, but it would have been nice to have said good-bye.

Sarah walked into the little house for the first time in nine months, and even though she knew that was not a long time, it had seemed like a lifetime. She made her way down the hall to her mother's bedroom as her father's voice boomed from behind her. "Katherine! Someone's here to see you!" When Sarah entered the room, her mother lit up with a big smile. "Sarah!"

She rushed into her mother's wide open arms, careful to avoid the cast on her wrist. "Oh, Mom! It's so good to see you." Both mother and daughter let the tears fall as they held on tight. "I love you so much."

"I love you, too, honey." Katherine pulled away and held Sarah at arms' length. "Let me look at you. Mmmmm…Hmmmm….I think American life is agreeing with you."

Sarah smiled as she leaned her mother forward and fluffed her pillow. "Yes, Mom. It's agreeing with me just fine. But I do miss my family." She observed the casted hand and foot. "I'm sorry this happened. Are you in any pain?"

"No. I've been well taken care of." She gave Sarah a wink as Mike came and stood in the doorway. "Just between you and me, I've got a crush on my doctor. He's soooo handsome."

Sarah chuckled. She didn't realize how much she had missed her parents. They were so happy in love, and for some reason, her mind went racing to David. She wondered where he was and what he was doing right now. There had been no time to say good-bye.

Katherine noticed her daughters far-away look. "Honey, are you okay?"

The front door slammed and Rebekah's footsteps came running down the hall, until she appeared with her face all aglow as she threw her arms around her sister, pulling her from her thoughts. "Sarah!"

"Rebekah!"

The two girls hugged and giggled. "I'm so glad you're home!"

"It's good to be home."

Mike stepped over to look at Katherine's leg while the girls enjoyed their reunion and picked up her water glass to get a fresh refill. "Okay, you two. I'm throwing you out. Your mother needs her rest."

Rebekah took the glass out of his hand. "Here, Dad. I'll do that."

Sarah took the glass from her sister. "No. I'll do it. You've been pulling quite a load around here, and it's time I do my share."

Katherine settled back onto the pillows and sighed. "It's so nice to have people fighting over me."

They all laughed as the two girls headed for the kitchen. Rebekah made a detour through the living room to straighten up the sofa pillows and fold an afghan while Sarah delivered the fresh water.

After Katherine was comfortable, Mike, Sarah, and Rebekah sat down on the front porch. Sarah looked at her dad with concern. "Okay, Dad. How is Mom, really?"

Mike sighed. "I think everything will heal back just fine, but she has a lot of swelling in her leg." He quirked an eyebrow. "You know your mother. She's not used to sitting still. Especially when there's work to be done for the Tent Revival meeting. But she's got to take it easy."

Rebekah draped an arm around her sister. "I know it must have taken quite a bit of organization for you to be able to come as quick as you did. It really means a lot, Sarah."

"I was planning to come home anyway. I just came a little earlier than planned. Tell me what I can do to help."

Mike leaned his elbows on his knees. "Well, if you can keep an eye on your mother and help Rebekah with the refreshments, I think your brothers can take care of everything else."

"In regard to the refreshments, how many are you planning for this year?"

Mike cleared his throat. "Around two hundred."

"Two hundred?!"

He took off his hat to wipe his forehead. "That's why we decided not to have a big meal, just a few refreshments. We simply can't afford to do more."

"Don't misunderstand, Dad. I'm excited that you're expecting such a great turnout."

"Getting them the gospel is the main thing. We've enjoyed seeing so many turn to Christ through this revival over the past few years. I'm praying for the Lord to bless again this year."

Sarah squeezed his arm. "I know he will."

Mike plopped his hat back on his head. "Well, I've got visits to make."

Sarah jumped to her feet. "Not without me."

He gave a lopsided grin. "I was hoping you'd say that. I thought you might want to visit Jose and Bianca. I've got to give Antonio his vaccinations today, and you might have to help us catch him. He's crawling now, and that little rascal is faster than a striped lizard."

Sarah turned to Rebekah with a pleading look and Rebekah laughed as she shooed her away. "Go ahead. I can manage."

Sarah popped a kiss on top of her head. "Thanks, Becksy!"

That evening, as Sarah sat in her spot at the dinner table, she looked around at the faces of her dear family. It was so good to be home. The rice, beans, and chicken were excellent. Rebekah had become as good a cook as Mother. Tim, Luke, and Micah had spent the morning hours visiting everyone in the village, reminding them of the upcoming meeting. They spent the remainder of the day hammering on the wooden platform that would be used as a stage. Up until this year, the guest speaker had simply stood at ground level, but the crowd had grown so large there was difficulty hearing and seeing from the back. When her brothers set their mind to something, there was nothing they couldn't do. Tim had also constructed a lectern while Micah put together a crude yet functional speaker system from spare parts of electronics and an old microphone he had found in one of the storage bins. Churches from the United States would send items from time to time, and what couldn't be used immediately was placed in storage for future use. Katherine knew Micah's flare for inventions, so she never threw away anything. When he was five, he had made a toy tank out of shoe boxes and paper towel rolls, and it just went from there. Rebekah had overseen the household affairs, taken care of Mother, and made out her menu for the refreshment table.

After a day of walking the old paths and making the rounds with her father, Sarah began to realize her exhaustion. In the short time that she had been in the States, she had grown accustomed to driving where she needed to go instead of walking, and it was beginning to show in her endurance...or lack thereof.

After dinner, the men folk headed out back to continue their work on the platform while Rebekah began clearing the dirty dishes from the table. Sarah checked on her mother and then returned to the kitchen to help her sister with the dishes.

"You don't have to help, Sarah. You've had a long flight and a tiring day. You must be exhausted."

Rebekah placed a wet plate into the dish drainer, and Sarah picked up a towel to begin wiping it down. "I want to help. That's what I'm here for. Though it looks like you guys have everything covered without me."

"Don't be silly. We've had to do without you, yes, but it certainly isn't our preference. It's so nice to have you home. How's Bianca and Baby Antonio doing today?"

Sarah smiled. "They're fine. And you were right. Antonio looks just like Jose. He's a pleasant little fellow, and Bianca seems well rested. She said that he was sleeping well at night."

Rebekah placed another dish and cup into the drainer. "Yes. He's a very good baby and blessed to have a wonderful mother. Bianca is so kind and patient with all her children." She chuckled. "Six boys. That takes the patience of Job."

Sarah joined her laughter and then they were silent for a moment in quiet thought, until Rebekah broke the silence. "Sarah, do you ever wonder if you will ever have children of your own someday?"

"I guess I've never really given it serious thought. I've been so occupied with medicine all my life that it hasn't been in the forefront of my mind."

"Do you ever think about the kind of man you would marry?"

Sarah's mind began to reel. Why was she suddenly thinking of Arizona? What was David doing right now? Where was he? The thought of him made her heart tighten. She had been wiping the same plate for the last few seconds, and now she not only wiped but also buffed, polished...

"Sarah?"

Sarah was abruptly pulled from her thoughts. "I'm sorry. What?"

Rebekah smiled and looked back down at the soapy water to begin on the final dirty cup.

"Who is he?" she asked softly.

Sarah's pulse raced. Rebekah had always seen through to her heart, but maybe she could play innocent. "He...who?"

"You're here beside me, but your mind is somewhere else. Where is it?"

She was going to try and side-step this one. "I was just thinking of a friend from Colorado."

"Dr. Barlow?"

"No."

"The new friend you mentioned. Elizabeth?"

"No."

Sarah could feel the heat rising to her face and tried desperately to tamp it down. If she blushed, Rebekah would know she was hiding something. It was a skill her sister had developed early in their childhood, and she had a way of always dragging out the truth.

Rebekah pulled out the drain plug and watched the dirty water swirl out of sight as she took the drying towel to wipe her hands. Sarah's mind raced for an answer. Maybe a subtle change of subject would work.

"Are we finished already? There were not as many dishes as I thought." Even as she said it, she knew Rebekah wasn't buying it.

"I've never seen you this nervous." She chuckled. "It *must* be a man."

Sarah took the towel out of Rebekah's hands and tossed it down on the counter as she shot her sister a side glance. "Who made you an authority on men?"

"I know you well enough to know that nothing rattles you. I've always admired your nerves of steel." Rebekah crossed her arms as her face broke into a wide grin. "So, the only thing I can think of that might actually shake your world is a guy. And I'm right, aren't I?"

Sarah rolled her eyes and sighed as she retrieved the dish cloth to give it a hearty wring. "Maybe."

Rebekah followed her into the dining room and watched, with her hands tucked in her apron pockets, as Sarah vigorously wiped down the table. "Maybe? That's all I get? You could at least tell me his name."

"Look, Rebekah. It's nothing really. He's just a friend."

"Oh, I think he's a lot more than just a friend."

"How would you know?"

Rebekah laughed. "Because this is the third time you've gone over that table. If you wipe it any harder, I'll have to get Tim to refinish it."

Sarah stopped abruptly and gave her sister a frustrated look as she took the cloth back to the sink. She stood with her hands on the counter, looking into the basin, when she felt Rebekah's hand on her shoulder. "I didn't mean to upset you. I'm just so happy for you."

Sarah shook her head. "Well, don't be happy for me. There's nothing to be happy about—at least not in that area of my life. When he looks at me, he only sees a friend of his sister and nothing more." She let out a shaky breath, and her voice softened. "I'm afraid that if I admit to myself that I really like him, I'll get hurt. Rebekah, I've spent a lifetime trying to avoid that kind of hurt. I promised God that I would wait on the one man he has for me. I've never been interested in playing the field because I don't want the baggage that goes with it. When I find the one man that God has for me to marry, I want to give him all of me, not broken leftovers."

"So, is this Elizabeth's brother we're talking about?"

Sarah's silence confirmed the answer. "Sarah, I don't know this guy, but if he overlooks you, he's crazy. Not to mention blind."

Sarah glanced up with a faint smile then back down at the sink. "You have to say that. You're my sister."

"Sarah, you're the most amazing person I know. Has he given you any indication of how he feels?"

"He's been kind and thoughtful, but I'm unsure of his motive." She sighed. "I don't really know what to think."

Rebekah put her arms around her sister and leaned her head to the side to touch Sarah's.

"I'll be praying for you."

Sarah rubbed her arm. "Thanks, Becksy."

Rebekah released her. "I'll check on Mom."

She walked out of the kitchen and then swung back around inside the doorway. "By the way, I guess you're still not going to tell me his name."

Sarah laughed as she threw the towel and plopped her sister upside the head. "You guessed right."

A ring sounded, and Luke came striding inside to retrieve it. A few moments later, the screen door screeched open, and Luke's voice boomed, "Dad! Telephone!"

Mike strode through the house to his office and closed the door. Sarah wanted to tell her dad good night, but it looked like it might be a few minutes, so she stretched herself on the sofa with one of the fluffy pillows to wait for the hug she wanted. The screen door opened again as her three brothers came bounding in. She could hear them bantering back and forth as they scrounged around the kitchen cabinets for a late night snack. Finally, Micah emerged with a piece of pie and a glass of milk. Luke had found a cookie. And Tim was nibbling a piece of cheese.

Sarah laughed. "Do you three ever get full?"

Micah cut the end off of his pie and stabbed it with a fork. "You gotta eat to keep from getting hungry."

Luke lifted her legs and rested them on his lap as he sat down on the sofa and propped his own feet on the little ottoman and took a bite of his cookie. "So, what do you think of the States?"

Tim sat down across from her. "Yeah. Are Americans as spoiled as everyone says they are?"

Sarah smiled at her brother's cynicism. "No. Not at all. It's just like anywhere else. You have the nice and the not-so-nice."

Micah asked with eyebrows bobbing up and down. "Have any nice guys spotted you yet?"

Sarah put a hand to her forehead. *Not again.*

Luke popped the last bite of cookie in his mouth. "They'd better keep their eyes to themselves if they know what's good for 'em."

Sarah didn't have to answer as she listened to her brothers go back and forth.

Tim finished off his cheese. "Sarah's got a good head on her shoulders. She can take care of herself." He leaned over to give her a hug. "Night, Sarah."

Luke moved from under her feet to slide over and give her a pop kiss on the head as he answered his brother. "I know she can take care of herself. I'm just saying that if she ever needs anyone to give a guy a sock in the head, I'm available."

Micah stepped over to give her a hug. "Those two could really use therapy." He popped a kiss on her cheek. "Night, sis."

Sarah laughed when the conversation continued as they made their way down the hall.

"Good night, Guys!"

They boomed out in unison. "Night!"

It was two hours later before Mike Phillips finally emerged from his office with a serious look as he swiped a hand down his face. He walked across the living room to head down the hall toward the bedroom when he spotted Sarah sleeping soundly on the sofa with a pillow tucked under her arms. He lowered himself into one of the chairs across from her to watch the slow, steady rise and fall of the pillow, and his mind went back to when she was a little girl. His chest tightened at the wonderful memories of his children. They had brought him and Katherine such joy. It was a blessing to see how God was using their lives to help others, and yet it was so hard to let them go. Parenthood was indeed bittersweet. *God, please take care of my little girl.*

Sarah stirred, squinted to open her eyes, and smiled. "I was waiting for my good night hug."

"Sorry, the phone call took so long."

She stood and stretched as she let out a yawn. "Everything is okay, I hope."

"Everything's fine."

Sarah noticed the tiredness around his eyes. "Are you sure?"

He gazed at her, studying his answer until he finally reached over to give her a big hug. "Night, Sarah."

His silence told her what she needed to know. He was concerned about something, but couldn't discuss it. She stood on tiptoes to wrap her arms around his neck. "Night, Dad. I love you."

His arms squeezed around her. "I love you, too, honey."

She watched his tired frame head for the bedroom, and an overwhelming love and appreciation for her father gripped her soul. He was everything a man should be. Godly, honorable, faithful, hardworking, and honest were just a few of his traits. He had set the bar high, and it was hard to imagine another man in the world even coming close. But there *was* such a man and thinking of him made her heart tight. *David, I wish I knew how you felt. Do you care for me as a friend or something more?*

Her pocket buzzed. She reached to pull out her phone and looked at the screen. She smiled. It was Elizabeth.

"Hi, Liz!"

"Hi, Doc! How are things in your half of the world?"

"Not bad, but a lot hotter."

"I hear ya. How's your mom? I hope I'm not calling too late."

"No. You could never call too late. Mom is moving slowly, but moving. How's Mr. Patrick?"

"Doing well. He likes the P.A. that's filling in for you, but says he isn't nearly as cute."

Sarah laughed as she pictured Peter with his wrinkled lab coat, his tousled hair, and his glasses on his nose. He was an excellent P.A. and very kind, but his crumpled appearance didn't exactly compliment his medical expertise.

"When will you be coming back?"

"In ten days, I hope."

"It can't come too soon for me. With you and Dave gone at the same time, I'm going crazy. By the way, have you heard from Dave?"

Sarah wished she could say yes, but, "Uh...no. I haven't."

"I'm surprised. He was pretty upset when he didn't get to see you before he left."

"I'm sorry. I hope it wasn't because I had to leave the party early."

"No. I told him what happened, and he was very concerned. It was so late that he decided to wait and talk to you the next day, but by then, you were on your way to Honduras. He hated that he missed you."

"When will he be back from Arizona?"

Liz gave a dismal, "Four weeks."

Sarah tried to keep the conversation upbeat to hide her disappointment. "Oh. Well, maybe I'll see him then."

She could hear Elizabeth's grin. "Yes. I'm sure you will. I know it's getting late, so I'll let you go. Talk to you later, and my best to your family."

"Thanks, Liz. Bye."

Sarah clicked off her phone and stuffed it back down into her pocket. She missed her friend, true. But she missed her friend's brother more. How pathetic was that? After she got back to Colorado, it would be about two more weeks before David was back. Then his schedule would be hectic, as baseball season would be officially in swing. It would be wonderful to see him, but she had a feeling that she would be taking a back seat in his life. It was probably for the best. She was getting too caught up in David, and that was a sure recipe for disaster. For all she knew, he might meet some nice girl in Arizona and totally blow her off when he got back. The thought of it made her sick and really didn't fit with his character. He was a sincere guy who wouldn't intentionally lead her on, but she had been wrong about people before. However, with David, she believed that he was everything he seemed to be…which was incredible.

Chapter Twenty-Three

Just three more to go. Two. One. David flopped back onto the mat, breathing hard and staring up at the florescent lights. Of all the exercises in the world, sit-ups had to have been invented by the Vietnamese as a form of torture. Every muscle in his body ached. He sat up and reached into his duffel for a bottle of water and gulped it down. Everyone else had already left the weight room, and the silence was golden. Since he had been in training, his mind had been occupied every minute of every day. And at night, he was so exhausted by the time he hit the rack, he was asleep almost instantly. But Sarah was tucked into his heart and mind. While he sat in the dugout waiting for an inning to end, she crossed his thoughts. When he spent time in prayer every morning, her image came vividly to his mind. Any idle moment was an opportunity for her to enter his thoughts. Amazingly, he had been able to focus on the job at hand, but she had been a pleasant distraction during the long weeks away from home. Home was always a warm thought. But Sarah brought more meaning to it. She would be back from Honduras by the time he returned to Colorado, and for the first time in a long time, he was truly homesick. His stomach churned. No, not homesick. Lovesick.

"I don't have to guess what you're thinking about."

David had been lost in his thoughts and didn't hear Steve come into the weight room. He got up off the floor and grabbed a towel from his bag to begin drying the sweat from his face. At least that's what he wanted his friend to think. In reality, he didn't want his expression to give away his thoughts, and a sweat towel on his face seemed to be the best option.

"I was just catching my breath. I'm ready to hit the showers and turn in."

Steve sat astride one of the weight benches. "Have you talked to her?"

Now would be a good time to play innocent. "Who?"

Steve grinned. "You know who."

"Liz?" David took another gulp of water and swished it around his mouth before swallowing.

Steve laughed at David's weak attempt to throw him off. "I just thought you could tell me how the weather is in Honduras this time of year."

"Hot." David shot Steve a grin as he headed for the showers. "Very hot."

Twenty minutes later, David emerged from the shower room and found Steve sitting in the same place he left him, curling a few reps with a dumbbell.

"So, when did you call her?"

David was totally caught off guard with the question. "Boy, when you hone in on a train of thought, you stick with it."

"I don't think you've called her at all. I would call you chicken, but that would be too second grade, and I might lose my job in the process."

David dropped his bag on one of the benches and sat down to pull a sweatshirt and pants over his shorts and T-shirt. "Okay, so I didn't call her."

Steve sat down the weight, walked over, and propped his size thirteen cowboy boot up on the bench. "You've been here for two weeks and you haven't called her?"

He reached down to pull on a sock, hoping to tamp down the loneliness that filled his chest. "Nope."

Steve grinned. "Mind if I call her?"

David pulled on the other sock. "Yep."

Steve chuckled and slapped him on the shoulder. "I'm kidding, man. But mind if I ask why you haven't talked to her?"

David narrowed his eyes, and he gave his friend a half grin. "Why are you so interested in this? You. A man who runs from relationships like your pants are on fire."

"We've been friends a long time. I've seen people try to fix you up with all kinds of women." He chuckled. "Do you remember that woman who fixed you up with her cousin? Let's see. What was her name again? Uh…"

David gave a bland reply. "Margaret. And don't remind me."

Steve started laughing. "Whew. That woman needed a red flag waving over her head." He turned serious. "But Sarah's different. And you don't really have to know her a long time to figure that out."

David blew out a sigh and leaned back against the cold block wall. "All right. You want the truth? She scares the socks off of me."

Steve howled in laughter. "What?"

Listening to Steve laugh, he couldn't help but laugh too. "It's true. I don't mean to sound like a jerk, but I've never had to work at getting a woman to notice me. It just comes with the territory. But with Sarah, it's different. She sees through all the bright lights, right down to the real me. She's looking for something more than a house, sports cars, fancy clothes, and plenty of money. She's everything I've been waiting for, and now that God has brought her into my life, I'm not sure how to handle it. I can't read her at all. I wish I had some idea of how she feels toward me."

Steve slapped him on the shoulder and sat down on the bench beside him. "Maybe that's just it. You've been so used to being in the driver's seat and in control that you've forgotten that you should let God be in control. If it's his will for you to be with Sarah, then he'll work it out. Both of you will have his peace that it's right."

David gave him an amused grin. "When did you get so smart?"

"I'm good at giving advice. I'm just not very good at taking it."

"Yeah, man. I can't wait to meet the woman who boils you over. Then, it'll be my turn to laugh at you."

Steve stood up straight. "You'll be waiting a lifetime for that one, buddy. I'm a confirmed bachelor, and I like it that way."

David grabbed his duffel and laughed as they walked toward the door. "That's what you say, but somewhere out there is a woman with your number."

Steve swung open the weight room door that led out into the hallway. "Well, if there was, I wouldn't wait two weeks to call her."

David winced. "Ouch."

Chapter Twenty-Four

David got back to his room and settled in for the night. He knew Steve was right. He needed to call her. But Steve was right about something else too. He was chicken, and he really didn't like that term. After some time on his knees in prayer, he threw back the covers and slid between the cool sheets. The digital clock on the hotel nightstand read nine thirty. It was too late to call. Her family probably turned in early. Besides, Honduras is one hour ahead, so that meant it was ten thirty where she was.

He stretched his arms back behind his head and tried to relax, but rest just wouldn't come. His cell phone chimed from inside the nightstand drawer. It was Liz.

"Hey, Liz."

"Hey yourself. Why haven't you called Sarah? I just talked to her, and when I asked her if she had talked to you, she said no."

David swiped his hand over his face. "I'm fine. Thanks for asking."

Liz got quiet for a moment. "I'm sorry, Dave. How are you?"

"All right. Just a little tired."

"Okay. Now. Why haven't you called Sarah?"

"Liz, I don't see where this is any of your concern."

"Of course, it's my concern. You're my brother, and she's my best friend."

"Look, I was thinking of calling her, but it's too late. I'm sure she's already gone to bed for the night."

"No, she hasn't. I just talked to her."

David got quiet as his chest tightened. "How was she?"

"Okay, I guess. She seemed a little down. Especially when I asked if you had called."

"Really?"

"Just look at it this way, Dave. If nothing else, Sarah could use a friend right now. She's under a lot of pressure. I'm sure she's torn between helping her family and coming back to her obligations here."

"I know."

"Look, I know you can take care of this without my help. Whether or not you like Sarah is between you and her. I just know that girls like Sarah don't grow on trees. She's for real, Dave. You can count on it."

"I know, Liz. I want to do the right thing."

"I'm sure that both of you do. I love you, and I just want to see you happy, Dave."

"Thanks, Liz. I love you too. And Liz? God loves you more."

"Night, Dave."

"Night."

He clicked off his phone and closed his eyes. *God, please help Liz.*

He opened his eyes, and his heart pumped hard at the thought of what he was about to do. He had made Sarah a matter of prayer during his time away from home, and his soul was completely at peace. He looked down at his phone and began scrolling through his contact list until he reached her name.

Sarah had just gotten up from the sofa to head to bed when her cell phone rang. A glance toward the mantle clock told her it was a little past ten thirty. It was unusual to get a call this late unless it was an emergency, so she grabbed the phone without taking time to look at the screen to identify the caller.

"Hello?"

"Hi, Sarah. It's David."

Sarah's pulse hit overdrive and her mouth went dry. She wanted to cheer and panic all at the same time. *Stay calm.*

"Hi, David. How are you?"

He winced when he looked at the clock. She sounded tired. "I'm fine. I hope I haven't called you too late."

She eased back down onto the sofa. "No, not at all. I tend to keep late hours. How are things in Arizona?"

"Going well. I'm sorry I haven't called before now. How's your mom?"

Sarah's tone was cheerful. "She's not used to being waited on hand and foot, so it's hard to make her rest, but she's okay. And don't apologize for not calling. I'm sure you've been pretty busy yourself."

"The hours are long, but I always enjoy spring training. I'm sure you've enjoyed being home for a few days."

Micah walked through the living room on his way to the kitchen and growled a low "I need a glass of water."

David heard a man's voice in the background and he tensed. "Do you need to go?"

Sarah giggled. "No. That was just Micah getting up for a glass of water. He's a bear when he has interrupted sleep." Micah stumbled through the living room on his way back to bed.

"Night, Sarah."

She slightly turned from the phone. "Night, Micah."

Sarah turned back to her caller. "It's been great being home. Since I didn't get to come home for Thanksgiving or Christmas, we're trying to make up for lost time. Last night, we had a big turkey dinner and exchanged Christmas presents."

David relaxed, slumped down into his covers, and put one hand behind his head on a plump pillow. "That sounds like fun. What did you get?"

"I got a homemade jewelry box from Tim, an umbrella from Luke, a stationary kit from Rebekah, and you'll never guess what I got from Micah."

David started laughing. "Oh no! I bet I can guess."

Sarah chuckled "He went out and caught a snake and put it in a glass jar with a beautiful red bow on top."

"Are you going to keep it?"

She lowered her voice so Micah wouldn't accidentally overhear. "Not hardly. I told him that snakes were against FFA regulations, so I would have to leave it behind, and he could take care of it for me. Mom and Dad got me a new stethoscope. It's awesome, and I needed a new one."

"Do I get to ask what you got them for Christmas?"

"I ordered them a new dining table that arrived yesterday. The old table was falling apart, so they were very pleased with a new one. I thought about getting something for everyone individually, but the more I thought about the table, it just seemed right."

"That was a great idea. I'm sure they appreciated it."

"It was an enjoyable belated Christmas. So, tell me about your training."

"There's really not much to tell. I jog and weight train in the morning, practice pitches all day, and play ball at night. The next day it starts all over again."

"How's Steve?"

"Restless, but good."

"I talked to Liz earlier. She said your dad is doing well."

"Yeah, she called me too. She has to annoy me at least once a day to be happy."

Sarah laughed. "Is that any way to talk about your sister?"

He chuckled. "Believe me, that's one of my nicer comments. But seriously, Liz is great. I couldn't do without her. If she didn't give me a hard time, I'd think she didn't like me anymore."

"I can't wait to see Liz. I miss her."

"When will you be back?"

"In about a week and a half. I don't feel like I can be away from the office any longer than that, even though I'm sure Peter is doing a great job in my absence."

David could feel the conversation coming to an end, but he couldn't bring himself to say good-bye. The nervous jitters had been replaced with an easy calm, but he could feel them climbing back into his chest. The momentary silence ended and the words came out. "I miss you, Sarah."

Her heart raced with the soft confession. "I miss you too."

"The day after I get home, I have a game. Will you be able to come?"

"I'll be there."

"Well, it's getting late and you need rest. I'll talk to you again soon. Is it all right if I text you?"

"Sure. And thanks for calling, David."

David settled under the covers. Not only had he survived the call, but he had ended up enjoying it. Sarah affected him that way. She was easy to talk to, and he could kick himself for not calling her sooner. She needed to know how much he cared. In just a few weeks, he would be back home in Colorado, and baseball season would be well underway. That would limit how much time he would have to see her, but he would find a way. He needed to talk to her face-to-face...and soon.

Sarah clicked off the phone and rested back on the sofa in the darkness, with only a faint light from the hall. She let out a shaky breath. He had called. Whether he meant it in friendship or something more, it meant so much. It was nice to hear his voice. When he said, he missed her, there had been sincere feeling that went straight to her heart. She missed him too. More than she wanted to admit.

Rebekah came into the room wrapped in her robe. "Are you all right?"

"Sure. I'm fine. I just had a phone call. I'm coming to bed."

Rebekah replied softly. "It was him, wasn't it?" More of a statement than a question.

Sarah looked down at her hands. "Yes."

"It was nice of him to call."

"Yes, it was. He called to see how Mom is doing."

Rebekah gave an amused grin. "Sure, he did."

Sarah's brow tensed. "What's that supposed to mean?"

Rebekah sighed as she sat down on the little ottoman in front of Sarah.

"He doesn't even know Mom. And even though I'm sure his inquiry was sincere, his interest was in you. Sarah, he obviously called because he cares about you. I don't want to give you false hope in this guy because I don't know him, but he must think very highly of you to have called from another country in the middle of the night."

Sarah shrugged one shoulder. "I'm sure he cares. He's just that kind of person."

"You're in denial. How many other women do you think he called tonight to see how their mothers were doing?"

Sarah laughed. "Has anyone ever told you that you have warped logic? Just because he was nice enough to call, you've decided he must be interested in me."

Rebekah smiled. "You're an easy person to love, Sarah, because you genuinely care about people unconditionally. Sounds like this mystery man of yours must see that too."

"I honestly don't know what he sees."

"Do you remember the night I called you, and you were upset and confused. I prayed with you, remember?"

Sarah nodded.

"Was it over this guy?"

She nodded again. "... and my concern for Elizabeth."

"I never knew what was bothering you, but I committed to pray for you every day and I'm still praying. Stop worrying and let God take care of this for you."

Sarah reached over to give her sister a hug. "Thanks, Becksy. I love you so much."

"I love you, too. Think you can get some sleep now?"

"I think so."

They stood to head for the bed when Sarah's phone rang a text.

Good night, Sarah. David

She held up the screen for Rebekah to see. "Well, so much for getting any sleep."

Rebekah smiled. "Hmmm…David. At least I know his name now."

Sarah slipped her phone down into her pocket when it jingled again. Rebekah put a hand to her head. "Another call? Who is it this time?"

Sarah looked at her phone and gave her sister a confused look. "It's Liz again. I hope everything is all right."

She clicked her phone. "Hi."

"I'm sorry to call again, but…I wanted to ask you something." Her tone was not the typical happy-go-lucky Liz.

"Sure."

Elizabeth was quiet for a moment. "You're a good person, Sarah. The most kind and honest person I know." She paused, and Sarah could feel in her soul what was coming. "So…why…do you think you need religion to go to heaven?"

Sarah motioned for Rebekah to come over to the sofa and she scribbled "*pray*" on a piece of paper. Rebekah gave her a knowing look and knelt beside the sofa as she went to the Lord in silent prayer.

"Well, Liz, the first thing you need to understand is the difference between God and religion. Most people think they are one and the same, but they're not. Religion is man-made. It's when man tries to get to God on his own terms. But God is God. He always has been, and he always will be. I believe the Bible to be the Word of God to man. It's a personal letter to us from God Almighty. He's given us instruction on how to go to heaven and how to live life, and it has nothing to do with our works."

"Yes. But there are many ways to get to heaven."

"The Bible says there is only *one* way. Jesus himself said, '*I* am the door. He also said, 'No man cometh to the Father, meaning God, but by Me, meaning Jesus."

"I'm not perfect, but I haven't killed anybody or anything. And, Sarah, I don't mean to be high and mighty, but I live better than most people I know who say they're a Christian."

Virtuous

"That may very well be true. There are many wolves in sheep's clothing. There are also Christians who are simply not living according to God's Word. But you can't compare yourself to another person. You must compare yourself to God and his holiness, then ask yourself how well you measure up."

Liz blew out a sigh. "That's a pretty tall order."

"Yes, it is. Romans 3:23 says that *all have sinned and come short of the glory of God.* The Bible tells us that God's son, Jesus Christ, came to this world to die on a cross for our sin because he loved us. God is holy and perfect. No sin can enter heaven and so, as sinners, we had no hope of ever going to heaven until Christ took the punishment of our sin for us. He was placed in a tomb, and three days later, he rose from the dead, conquering death for us. Did you know that there were more witnesses of Christ being alive after the crucifixion, than witnesses for the signing of the Declaration of Independence? He lives, Liz. We are not perfect or sinless, but because Jesus took our punishment, God will now accept us into his presence for Jesus's sake. Jesus said, he is the *only* way to heaven. He said, 'I am the way, the truth, and the life.' If we reject Jesus, God will reject us. We can never be good enough. If we could, then Jesus's death on the cross was in vain."

Liz got quiet again. "I'll think about it."

"Think about one more thing. Do you believe the Bible is true?"

"Yes. I think it's true."

"Do you have a Bible close by?"

"Yes. I've been looking through it."

"Go to the book of Luke. Chapter 23, verses 42 and 43."

Sarah could hear Liz rustling the pages. "Got it."

"Now, this passage is about when Jesus was on the cross. He was hanging between two thieves. One of the thieves was making fun of him, but look at what the other said."

Liz began reading. "And he said unto Jesus, Lord, remember me when thou comest into thy kingdom. And Jesus said unto him, Verily I say unto thee, Today shalt thou be with me in paradise."

"You see, Liz? This man was a common thief, hanging on a cross for his crime. There wasn't any time for him to be good to his neighbor or give to his favorite charity. He wasn't good enough to go to heaven, and yet Jesus said that he would be with him in paradise. The thief simply believed that Jesus was who he said he was...the son of God. Believing on Jesus Christ is faith. It's believing even when you can't see. We were made by an awesome creator. We didn't just happen. We are here by divine design with a purpose."

Liz was quiet for a moment, and then she sighed. "I know it's late, and I need to let you get some sleep. I appreciate you talking with me."

"Any time."

"Night, Sarah."

"Night, Liz."

Sarah slid down onto her knees beside Rebekah and let the tears flow.

Rebekah put an arm around her shoulders. "She's asking questions. That means she's thinking about it. That's good, Sarah."

"I know. I just pray that God will mercifully keep her safe until she believes on him."

Chapter Twenty-Five

Elizabeth curled her feet up under the covers of her bed and looked down at the open Bible. David had mentioned a verse to her a few weeks ago. He wrote it down on a card and stuck it inside the Bible. She flipped to the front, where it read: To Liz, from Dave. May God show you his wonderful love.

She finally found the little card with the scripture Dave had written on it. It was tucked in the book of Ephesians. Liz flipped over to the reference: Ephesians 2:8–9.

For by grace are ye saved through faith; and that not of yourselves: it is the gift of God: Not of works, lest any man should boast.

Elizabeth's heart pounded as she whispered. "That's what Sarah was talking about."

She went back to the scripture about the thief on the cross and backed up to the beginning of the chapter. Luke 23. Her eyes followed down the page until she landed on the words of Pilate, "I find no fault in this man." Her hands began to tremble as she felt the sorrow of Jesus's death sentence and crucifixion. Then she read where Jesus spoke while hanging in agony on the cross, "Father, forgive them; for they know not what they do."

The tears began to flow, and she chided the words on the page. "But he was innocent. Pilate said so himself." Elizabeth remembered the words of Bro. John Hawks when he had spoken at one of her mother's Bible studies. He spoke of the cruel and brutal nature of crucifixion. The crown of thorns on his head and the spikes in his hands and feet. All this was after he had been brutally beaten by the Roman soldiers. Elizabeth's mind raced. *He was in unspeakable pain and yet he asked God, his father, to forgive us? To have mercy? If there was any other way to heaven, surely God would not have allowed his only son to endure such torture on my behalf.*

The truth shined into Elizabeth's soul as she fell to her knees at the bedside. "Oh, God! Please forgive me for rejecting your son. He suffered cruel punishment for my sake. I know now that I could never do anything to earn heaven. I believe on Jesus Christ to be my savior. Amen."

Elizabeth's tears of sorrow turned to tears of relief and joy as the forgiveness of a holy God washed over her soul. She grabbed a tissue from the nightstand and crawled back into bed, but she was too excited to sleep. It was too late to call Sarah or Dave. She would wait for the right time to tell them.

Chapter Twenty-Six

The time with family had passed quickly. Sarah pulled back into her parking space behind the office building and turned off the ignition. David would be back tomorrow. He had called a couple of times since she had been back from Honduras, and the conversations had been short. But every evening around eight o'clock, he would text. *Thinking of you, David.* She would appreciate his thoughtfulness and leave it at that. It would be wonderful to see him again, but the thought of seeing him completely unnerved her. What would he say? What should *she* say? She couldn't think of a thing, and she wasn't even face-to-face with him yet. It seemed impossible to become closer to someone while they were hundreds of miles away, but it had happened. She clicked the release on her seatbelt and began gathering her belongings to head into work when her cell rang. She noted the screen. It was him.

"Hello?"

"Morning. Did I catch you before you got to work?"

She smiled. "Just barely. I'm in the parking lot getting ready to go in. How are you?"

"Homesick. I can't wait to taste Maria's beef stew. I've already put in my order for tomorrow night."

Sarah giggled. "I think she spoils you."

"Sure she does. She needs someone to spoil, so it should be me."

"What time will you be getting in?"

"My plane doesn't land until around eight o'clock tomorrow night."

"That beef stew is going to be more like a midnight snack."

"I've got a game the next day, so I'll work it off."

He got quiet for a moment. Then, "That's why I was calling. Are you still planning to come to the game on Friday?"

"Absolutely. I wouldn't miss it. I've never been to a game before."

"I've got one of the visitor suites reserved."

"Oh, I see. Is this another party like before? If so, I'll be glad to help out with Mr. Patrick."

"Uh...no. Mom and Dad won't be there, and neither will Liz. They have plans to attend a charity benefit tomorrow night."

"Well, I guess I'll have to cheer extra hard to make up for their absence. Is it in the same suite as before?"

"No. It's a smaller one farther down the corridor. Steve knows to keep a look out for you. I'll send a ticket to your office tomorrow with directions. The game starts at 7:00 PM."

"I may be a little late, but I'll be there."

"Sounds great. I'll see you after the game."

"All right. Have a safe trip home."

"Thanks."

"Bye, David."

"Bye."

She clicked off her phone and sat for a moment. He sounded happy, well, and excited about the upcoming game. Since she would be meeting him in the visitor suite, maybe it wouldn't be so awkward after all. There would be lots of people there like before, and it would take some of the pressure off. It had been a bit nerve-racking the first time, but now that she knew some of the players and their families, it would be much more comfortable. Steve would be there too, so maybe he could help educate her on the finer points of baseball.

She gathered her belongings, stepped out, and hit her keyless entry. As she started across the parking lot, her phone jingled again. When she reached her office, she pulled out her cell to read the text. *PS. I miss you.*

She closed her door, dropped her bag into the floor, and sank into the big office chair. *Lord, should I reply or not?* She took a shaky breath and tapped, *I miss you too.*

Thinking that was the end of conversation, she tried focus on one of the memos lying on her desk as she pulled on her lab coat and threw her new stethoscope around her neck. She was tugging her long hair out from underneath her coat collar when her phone jingled again. *Postgame will be semi-formal.*

She tapped back. *Thanks for the tip.*

Friday was busy, and it kept Sarah's mind totally occupied. Mrs. Mason brought in little Gracie for her three-month shots, Mr. Daggett had broken a foot by falling from a roofing job, and ten-year-old Tyler had strep throat. Thankfully, the flu season had subsided, and there had been no emergencies. For the first time in days, she headed to her office for a quiet lunch. The chicken noodle soup and cold-cut sandwich looked and smelled great. The office didn't reopen for patients until two o'clock, so there was plenty of time to relax. With her office door open, she could hear the television in the employee lounge. It was on a local news channel that was covering the big Wolves game tonight, so she picked up her cup of soup and stepped into the lounge to hear the latest.

The sportscaster was announcing the game with a picture of David boxed in the corner of the screen.

"David Patrick will be starting the game tonight against the Cobras. His coach says he's ready and at the peak of his career."

The screen switched to a brief interview in the locker room, showing David seated on a wooden bench in a Denver Wolves T-shirt. "We've been working hard during spring training, and we're looking forward to a great season."

The announcer interrupted, "You can catch the game on this station tonight at 7:00pm."

Sarah picked up the remote, flipped off the television, and headed back for her sandwich; but her appetite was gone. After seeing him on the screen, she was way too nervous to eat. Millie knocked on the door and stuck her head in.

"Someone dropped this off for you."

Sarah took the little white envelope. "Thanks, Millie."

She opened it and found her game ticket along with directions and the handwritten note, *I miss you.* She missed him too. But seeing him on television brought back the reality of her situation. He would never be interested in her. During her short time in the States, she had learned that guys like that went for Hollywood actresses or other famous athletes. Not wallflowers.

When two o'clock rolled around, Dr. Barlow had to leave and head to the hospital to attend to one of his patients who had an emergency. So, Sarah and Pete took care of their load as well as Dr. Barlow's. At six o'clock, she finally locked the back office door behind her and rushed out to her car. Why did this always happen? David said this was a semiformal event and she would have to go home and change. The plan was to leave the office at four so she would have plenty of time, but she should have known better than to have counted on that happening. Well, it couldn't be helped. She would just get there as soon as she could. If the crowd was as large this time as it was for the last party, she could easily slip in unnoticed.

Traffic was murder. At seven thirty, she was still stuck in a jam and decided to turn on the radio to hear the game. The Wolves were up 2-0 in the bottom of the third inning. Traffic began to move, and she finally made it to Blake Street. The parking lot was a sea of automobiles. She pulled out the ticket that had directions stapled onto the back and found the VIP parking spot.

As she ascended the flights of stairs and walked down the crowded corridor, she passed several food vendors, and the smell of buttery popcorn was in the air. People were everywhere. Most of them were wearing the team colors and jerseys. One little girl had a wolf painted on her face.

Sarah looked down at her ticket again and carefully began studying the letters and numbers displayed on the stadium walls. Something was wrong. She needed to go up another flight. When she finally reached the next level, the crowd didn't seem to be quite so thick. Following the letters all the way to the end, she noticed Steve, standing by the door at the end of the walkway.

He tipped his big cowboy hat. "Hey, Doc."

Sarah gave him a big grin. "Steve!" She walked over to shake his hand. "You're a sight for sore eyes."

Steve covered her hand with his big one. "I was beginning to think you weren't coming."

She chuckled. "Me too. How have you been?"

Steve crossed his arms. "Busy. It's a full-time job keeping Dave out of trouble, you know."

She gave him an amused grin. "You certainly have your hands full. I hope he pays you well."

He smiled back. "Not nearly enough, ma'am."

Sarah laughed. "Have I missed the game completely?"

"Oh no, ma'am. The Wolves are batting in the bottom of the fourth. We just scored another run. We're up three to zip."

He swiped his card on the keyless door lock and pulled open the door. Sarah stepped inside a beautifully decorated private suite. The lights were dim—and not a soul was present.

Steve spoke from behind her in his finest Texas drawl. "Somebody else'll be joining you after a bit."

She whirled around and opened her mouth to ask what was going on. This couldn't be the right place. Maybe it was the wrong room. But Steve just gave her a knowing smile and tipped his hat as he eased back out the door. "I'll be right outside if you need anything, ma'am." And he was gone.

Chapter Twenty-Seven

Sarah wandered around the room, completely in awe. Next to the huge glass windows sat a small table for two that overlooked the field. The centerpiece was a huge bouquet of yellow roses surrounded by tiny, white blooms of baby's breath and a card that simply read "Sarah."

She stepped over to the window overlooking the game. The Wolves were just taking the field for the top of the fifth inning. She could see David walking up to the mound in his white uniform, tossing the ball hard in his glove and adjusting his hat. It was hard to make out his features, but she was sure it was him. Number fifteen.

The first batter for the Cobras stepped up to the plate, and David leaned in with his hands behind his back to take the signal from the catcher. He nodded and straightened as he held his glove and ball in front of his face, ready for the wind up. He lunged and threw. Strike one! The crowd cheered! The catcher threw the ball back to David, and he made his way back to the mound. Same pitch. Strike two!

An organ sounded and the crowd yelled, "Charge!" Sarah looked around the stadium. It was full to capacity, and she was amazed at so many fans wearing a Wolves jersey with the number fifteen. Strike three! The crowd went wild! She couldn't help but clap and cheer as the frustrated batter returned to the dugout.

Sarah's phone jingled, and she reached in her pocket. The screen displayed a number that she wasn't familiar with.

She wrinkled her brow. "Hello?"

"Hello. Is this Dr. Phillips?"

"Yes, it is. Who's calling, please?"

"This is Martha Martin."

"Oh! Hello, Mrs. Martin. I'm sorry I didn't recognize your voice. How are you?"

"I'm fine, dear. I hope I haven't caught you at a bad time."

"No, not at all. What can I do for you?"

"I was calling to ask your advice on something."

Sarah expected a medical question. "I'll certainly be glad to help any way that I can."

"Well, I was talking to Mary the other day, and she was telling me what a great seamstress you are. She seems to know a lot about you since you spend so much time at their home. Anyway, Elsie has a wedding gown already, but she's going to need bridesmaid dresses, of course. I was wondering if you would be willing to make the dresses or would know of someone who could make them, if you don't have time. I guess we could just buy them, but Elsie wanted something unique and special."

"I'm afraid I wouldn't have time, and I haven't lived here long enough to know of anyone else. I'm sorry, Mrs. Martin. But I'm happy for Elsie. I didn't know she was engaged."

"Really? I'm surprised, since you seem to be so cozy with the Patrick's."

Sarah disregarded the smug remark. "No. They haven't mentioned it. Who is Elsie's fiancé?"

"Why, David, of course."

Sarah felt her legs turn to water as she slowly lowered herself into a nearby chair. Her mind froze, but she had to say something. All she could think of was, "I didn't know."

Martha twittered a high-pitched giggle. "Well, I won't keep you. If you think of anyone who could make the dresses, just let me know. But don't say anything to Mary. I wouldn't want to bother her with the details. She already has such a big responsibility looking after Jack."

"No, ma'am."

"Good-bye, dear."

"Bye."

Sarah took a shaky breath. She felt like she had been sucker punched in the gut. The feeling made her sick. None of this made sense. Or did it? All of the pep talks she had given herself over the last few months had been accurate. He was just being a nice guy. Probably for Elizabeth's sake. He really *did* call Honduras to check on her mother. For all of the care she had taken to guard her heart, she had still gotten hurt. It hurt like nothing else she had ever experienced in life. The cheers of the crowd were just a dull sound as she sat lifeless in the room all alone, staring into the memories of the past days and weeks. How could she have been so foolish? Even though she had not revealed her feelings to anyone, not even Rebekah, she was embarrassed and ashamed. She knew he would never be interested in someone like her. Sarah dropped her face into her hands.

Lord, how could I have let this happen? When I should have been completely focused on the children's home and my medical responsibilities, I let myself get distracted. I even allowed myself to think that he cared. God, you know my thoughts and the intents of my heart. I can hide nothing from you. I confess, my heart is in pieces. Please help me. The tears welled, but she refused to let them fall. Surely, God would grant her the grace to face this evening.

The rest of the ballgame passed without notice as Sarah sat in stunned despair. And the dread of facing David was overwhelming.

David stood in front of the mirror in the locker room and adjusted his tie.

One of his teammates let out a low whistle. "Looks like Patrick has big plans."

Another teammate chimed in. "It's either a real hot date or a real late funeral." The locker room erupted in laughter. David just chuckled as he headed for the door. "Later, fellas."

Howls and whistles followed him out the door.

As he approached the VIP suite, the nerves got worse. How could a person look forward to something and dread it all at the same time? He couldn't wait to see her, but he also couldn't help but wonder what she had thought about his text messages. She had responded, so that had to be a good sign. But Sarah was hard to read. That was just the price a man paid, to fall for a got-it-together kind of girl.

He finally reached the top of the stairs and spotted Steve guarding the door. As he approached, Steve's grin got bigger.

"Lookin' sharp, man."

David gave him a nervous grin. "I don't feel so sharp. Is she here?"

"Yep. Been here since the bottom of the fourth."

"Well, at least we won. I'd hate to do this on a loss."

Steve smiled. "The waiter brought up your dinner about five minutes ago. If you feel like eating, that is."

David gave him a frustrated glance. "I think you're enjoying this."

Steve chuckled again and crossed his arms. "And I think you're stalling."

He let out a long sigh, reached for the door, and Steve grabbed his arm. "I don't wanna make you more nervous, but she looks amazing."

David gave him a side glance and a bland "Thanks."

Sarah was standing next to the table looking out the window when she heard the suite door open. She could see his reflection in the glass as he walked into the room. He looked fabulous. All six-foot-plus of him in a sharp black suit. The sick feeling that she had managed to get under control had returned. She knew she had to face him. Taking a deep breath, she turned around.

David took her hands in his. Steve was right. She looked absolutely amazing in a soft pink sweater with multicolored skirt to match. Her long, blond hair curled down her back and around her shoulders. He smiled down at her. Then something hit him that something was wrong. Dreadfully wrong. He could see it in her eyes. She wasn't smiling, and he could feel her hands trembling beneath his. He could read the concern on her face. This was not the meeting he had been hoping for. He reached into his mind for something to say.

"It's good to see you."

She gave an expressionless nod.

He tried to think of a reason. Maybe she had a bad day at work. "Are you all right? I hope

you've had a good day."

She looked down at their hands joined together and quickly moved them.

"Yes. It was fine." Her answer was low and dismal.

It was getting late, so she had to be hungry. Hunger was a problem he could solve. But something told him that was not the problem. He guided her over to the table and pulled out her chair. "I hope you're hungry."

Looking down at her plate, she had yet to look him in the eye. This was not going well. "Yes. Thank you."

After eating in silence through the salad and most of the main course, she finally looked out the window, overlooking the field. "Congratulations on your win."

He gave a frustrated and simple "thanks" as he dug his fork into the green beans.

Sarah's mind was reeling. She was sitting here with David, an engaged man, having an intimate dinner with roses in the middle of the table addressed to her. This was unbelievable. How could she have been so wrong about him? She had fallen for a man that was completely different from what she believed him to be. And what about Elsie? She surely didn't know that her fiancé was having dinner with another woman tonight. Suddenly, she felt so cheap, like…the woman in the book of Proverbs that King Solomon warned his son about. Eating dinner was like choking down vinegar and sour grapes. She prayed all through dessert. *Lord, what do I do? What do I say to get out of this mess?*

When dessert was over and the waiter had taken away the cart of dishes, she rose from the table.

"Mr. Patrick, thank you for dinner, but I think I should go now."

David rose from his chair stunned. "Go? Now?"

"Yes."

She started past him to retrieve her coat when he caught her arm. "Sarah, I don't know what's going on, but something is terribly wrong. Did I offend you in some way?"

His mind went to the text messages; "I miss you," but she had returned the message, so that couldn't be it.

Sarah fell silent. She didn't make a move as his hand gently held to her arm.

He turned her toward him and she looked at the floor. He tilted her face where she had to look him in the eye. "What is it?" he pleaded.

Sarah looked into his dark, sincere eyes and wished she could have all the things that were in her heart. She took a shaky breath and looked away from him as she chided herself. This man belonged to someone else. He moved his hands to hold her face, but she pulled away. He had no right to be so intimate with her, and she must tell him so.

"Mr. Patrick, I appreciate your kindness, but you have no right to do this."

David felt the impact of her words, and it hit with force. She must belong to someone else. The words came out slowly. "I'm sorry, Sarah. I didn't know there was someone else in your life."

She narrowed her eyes. "In *my* life? Mr. Patrick, there's no one in my life. But I *do* know about *your* engagement."

David put his hands on his hips looking confused. "*My* engagement?"

She was calm but firm. "I know all about it. Mrs. Martin told me. And I don't feel that it's right for me to be here with you like this, when you and Elsie are engaged."

David looked at her in disbelief until his face broke into a grin and then hysterical laughter. "*Me*? Engaged to Elsie Martin? Come on, Sarah. Give me a little credit."

Sarah's expression was unchanged. "This isn't funny. I'm sure Elsie wouldn't appreciate you having dinner with me tonight."

David's laughter had softened to a low chuckle. "I really don't care what Elsie *or* her aunt appreciates."

Sarah blew out a sigh and began pulling on her overcoat. David pulled the coat off as fast as Sarah was trying to put it on. His demeanor had turned serious. He turned her toward him and held up a finger. "Wait."

After tossing her coat back onto the nearby sofa, he walked to the door and opened it for Steve to enter the room. David brought Steve over to where Sarah was standing and stuffed his hands into his suit pants pockets.

"Steve, I was wondering if you could clear something up for us."

Steve gave a confused look between them and let out a slow, "S-sure."

"Am I engaged?"

Now Steve was looking *really* confused. "Come again?"

David looked straight into Sarah's eyes as he asked Steve again. "Am I engaged?"

"No."

When David saw the belief in Sarah's eyes he dismissed Steve with a pat on the back. "Thanks, buddy."

Steve, still looking totally confused, walked back out of the room as he tossed back, "Sure," and began mumbling to himself as he closed the door behind him.

Sarah put a hand to her head, walked over to the window, and sighed, "I don't understand this."

David came up behind her to ask softly. "How in the world did you ever think I was engaged to anyone?" He shook his head. "Especially Elsie Martin?"

Sarah wrapped her arms around her waist. "You see, I was here watching the game when I got a phone call from Martha. She started asking me about making bridesmaids dresses for Elsie's wedding. I told her I didn't know Elsie was getting married and asked who she was engaged to. And…"

The emotions that Sarah had fiercely held down all evening caught in her throat. It was just too much. Her eyes welled, and a single tear made its way down her cheek as she took a shaky breath.

"She said Elsie was engaged to you."

David watched another tear make its way down her cheek, and he felt horrible for having laughed at her now. She was trembling, and he wrapped her in his arms.

"I'm so sorry for all this." He held her close and she could hear the pounding of his heart in her ear. "This was not what I wanted this night to be."

She wiped the tears and looked up at him. "I'm sorry too. You went to all this trouble…the dinner, the flowers…and I was so rude to you. I should have known you couldn't have done…what I thought." She shrugged her shoulders and shook her head. "I just didn't know what to think."

He took her face in his hands, and he was trembling. He gazed into her eyes. "That's my fault. I want to make it clear to you tonight how I feel so there are no more mistakes. I love you, Sarah. I love you more than I can ever put into words. You are the most amazing person I've ever known. I can only hope that you feel the same."

She looked into his warm gaze and saw her future with him as his words slowly eased into her mind. He was everything.

"I love you, too, David."

As she spoke the words, fireworks began illuminating the sky over the stadium. He turned to look. "Ever seen fireworks before?"

Sarah looked on in amazement as another explosion of color took to the sky. She smiled for the first time all evening. "No. They're beautif...?"

Her heart stopped, and then raced on. When she turned back to David, he was down on one knee, and she caught her breath. He opened a little blue velvet box displaying a ring of diamonds with a lovely red ruby in the center.

"Sarah Phillips, will you marry me?"

She stared for a moment then ran the back of her hand down his strong face as another tear trickled down her own. "Yes. I'll marry you, David."

He took the ring from the box and placed it on her finger. "This was my grandmother's."

"It's beautiful."

He stood and kissed her forehead then her nose and breathed, "Not as beautiful as you," and placed his lips to hers. Sarah was lost in his love. Words could not describe the love she felt for him. It was bliss to know that she would never have to bury her love for him again.

She pulled away and caught her breath. "There's just one thing."

He held her face in his hands. "What?"

"I can't officially accept your proposal until you've asked my father."

David's face broke into a knowing smile and Sarah's eyes widened. "You mean you've already asked him?"

"Do you remember the first time I called you when you were in Honduras? I talked to your dad that evening and asked his permission." He chuckled. "I had to go to the weight room and do about a thousand sit-ups just to work up the nerve to call you after that. It even took a little prodding from Steve."

She wrinkled her brow. "So, you were the two-hour phone call? He never said a word!"

David laughed. "He wasn't supposed to. I really like your dad. He gave me the third degree, but I expected that. Any father who loves his daughter would be concerned about who she marries. He asked me every question he could think of and then some."

Sarah sighed and hugged him close. "I love you, David. Thank you for honoring my father by asking his permission."

He whispered in her ear and breathed in her sugary fragrance. "How soon can I make you Mrs. Patrick?"

She pulled back to look into his eyes with a smile. "As soon as I can get my family here and do a little planning. How does two weeks sound?"

He leaned his forehead to hers. "About one week and six days too long."

"Sorry, but I think that's the best I can do."

He smiled. "Then I'll take it."

She sat down on the plush sofa overlooking the stadium and pulled him down with her. "So, what did Mr. and Mrs. Patrick, and Liz think of all this when you told them?"

David scratched his head. "Well, I haven't exactly told them yet."

Sarah's brows lifted. "You mean they don't know? When do you plan to tell them?"

He smiled at her. "I was sort of hoping you might like to have a little fun."

She quirked an eyebrow. "What are you up to, David Patrick?"

Chapter Twenty-Eight

Saturday morning, Sarah made arrangements to meet Elizabeth for a round of tennis. After an hour of volleying, they made their way back to the house for some brunch, compliments of Maria. The Western omelet, accompanied by bacon and fresh fruit was delicious. But Sarah's stomach was tied in too many knots to truly enjoy the meal, and Elizabeth took notice.

"I can't believe how little you've eaten. You're not getting sick, are you?"

Sarah gave her a weak smile. "No. I'm just not very hungry."

"Well, in that case..." Elizabeth reached over with her fork and stabbed a strawberry. "By the way, how's your mom? You haven't mentioned her in a couple of days."

"She's moving around a little better."

Elizabeth eyed her friend. "Hmmm...no appetite, accompanied by very little conversation. What's with you today?"

"Nothing, I'm fine."

"No, you're not. I know you well enough to know when you're fine and when you're not. And you're definitely not fine."

Sarah finished her orange juice. "That was excellent, Maria. Thank you." Maria took her plate and smiled.

"Well, I need to go and check on your dad. By the way, where is Mrs. Patrick?"

"She's with Dad." Elizabeth called after Sarah as she headed for the back patio. "Wait a minute! You're not spilling the beans! What's going on?"

Sarah called behind her as she made her way into the foyer. "Come on. You can go with me. You might learn something."

Elizabeth gave a bland, "Very funny."

They reached the great room, and Sarah pulled open the sliding glass door that led outside to the stone patio. She grinned at Elizabeth. "I might even let you use my new stethoscope."

Elizabeth rolled her eyes. "Gee, I can't wait."

Sarah pooched out her lip as she teased. "I thought you'd be excited. Stethoscopes are fun! Think of it as a cool kind of cell phone. You do all the listening. No talking."

"No talking? No way. I couldn't deal with that." Elizabeth spotted David coming up the steps from the garage. "Hey, I thought you had a team meeting this morning?"

David met them at the patio door. "I did, but I left a little early." He turned to Sarah. "I really need to talk to Mom and Dad. How long will you be?"

Sarah gave him a serious look. "Oh, not long. About thirty minutes should do it."

He blew out a sigh and raked a hand through his hair. "All right, I'll wait. I'll go and see if Maria had anything left over from brunch. I didn't have time for breakfast this morning, and I'm starving. I'll be back in thirty."

Elizabeth crossed her arms as she watched him go into the house. "Something's bothering him today. He seems tense. I hope nothing happened at the team meeting. I've never seen him so nervous."

Sarah stepped out to the patio with her sweet smile. "Good morning!"

Mary was tucking a quilt around Jack. "Good morning, Sarah! How was tennis?"

Elizabeth flopped down in a chair. "She's getting better all the time. If she keeps improving, I'm going to stop teaching her or she'll beat me."

Sarah moved a chair up beside Mr. Patrick. "And how's my favorite patient doing?"

Jack lit up with a smile. "I'm wonderful, now that all of my favorite gals are here with me."

It was great to hear him speak so clearly. God had truly performed a miracle in his life by restoring him back to good health. Sarah smiled as she gently took his wrist to get a pulse count. She had come to love this family as her own over the past few months. It was all she could do to contain her joy. She lowered his wrist back down and tucked it under the light quilt that Mary had provided. She took out her stethoscope and listened to his heart and lungs. Her back was to the door when David came out to join them. Liz studied his face. It was even more tense and serious.

"Morning, Dad."

"Morning, Dave."

He placed a loud kiss on Mary's cheek. "Morning, Mom."

"Good morning, dear."

"Are you about finished, Doc? I'd like to talk to my family in private."

Elizabeth gave him a frustrated look. "Dave, that was rude. What's wrong with you?"

Sarah put a hand on Elizabeth's arm. "It's okay. He obviously has something very important on his mind." She turned to David, away from everyone else, and gave him a wink. The corner of his mouth twitched, but he held a solemn expression. Sarah stuffed her stethoscope back into her bag. "I'll just be on my way. Thanks for the tennis, Liz. I'll talk to you later." And she stepped back inside the house.

When Sarah was gone, Elizabeth turned on him. "I can't believe you did that! You'd better have a good reason for insulting her."

Mary joined in. "Yes, Dave. That really *was* uncalled for. That young lady has been a God-send and a wonderful blessing to our family. She's done a lot for your father."

David had crossed his arms, but his hand went up to discretely cover his mouth. He wanted to laugh. At least he didn't have to guess what his family thought of Sarah. He gained his composure and put his hands on his hips as he let out a long sigh. Elizabeth realized that she might have been too hasty. Something was obviously bothering him or he wouldn't have sent Sarah away. He was one of the good guys. He wouldn't do such a thing without a very good reason.

She stepped over to him and put her hand on his arm. "Is everything all right, Dave? I'm sorry I snapped. You've been nervous all morning."

"There's something I need to tell all of you and I'm a little nervous about it."

Jack sat up farther in his chair, and Mary cocked her head to one side with a concerned look. She tried to ease his nerves. "It's okay, honey. Just tell us what's on your mind."

"Well, you see, I met this girl. I've known her for a short time and uh..." Elizabeth's brow wrinkled and she crossed her arms. "You didn't tell me anything about this. Who is she? What do you know about her?"

"I know she's a Christian. I've never met her family, but I've talked to her dad on the phone, and he seems like a real nice guy."

Elizabeth glared. "*Seems* like real nice guy?! I thought you said you've never met him. How do you know what kind of a guy he is?! And as far as this *Ms. Wonderful* being a Christian, that's what they all say. C'mon, Dave. You know better than to fall for that line. Now I know why you wanted Sarah to leave. You had someone else..."

Mary interrupted. "Liz, let your brother talk." Elizabeth plopped back down in her chair and stared at the floor.

David continued. "Anyway, I just wanted you to know that...I love her, and I've asked her to marry me."

Elizabeth's eyes got wide. "You did what?! Has she given you an answer? Please tell me she said no."

David grinned. "She said yes."

Elizabeth looked over at her mother. "Can you believe this?"

Mary was tense but calm as she eyed her son. "Liz, David is a grown man. He can make up his own mind about who he wants to marry." She cocked an eyebrow. "But I do wish we could have at least met her before he popped the question."

David bent down beside his mother's chair. "I do want you to meet her. In fact, she's here. I asked her to come here today so that I could introduce her to you, Dad and Liz."

Now Elizabeth was exasperated. "She's here?! Now?!"

David walked over to the door. "Yes. She's waiting inside. And Liz...*try* to be civil. She's your future sister-in-law."

He stepped inside the door and as he disappeared, Liz called out, "Can you at least tell us *Ms. Wonderful's* name?"

David reappeared in the doorway holding Sarah's hand, both of them smiling. "It's Doctor Sarah Phillips."

Elizabeth jumped out of her chair and wrapped her friend in a big hug. "Oh, I hoped it would happen! I *knew* it would happen!"

Sarah laughed. "In that case, I wish you would have told me."

Mary walked over to Sarah and took both of her hands. "Jack and I have prayed since the day that our children were born, that God would give them a wonderful person to share life with. I can't think of anyone that I have more trust and confidence in than you." She leaned to give Sarah a hug and David a kiss on the cheek.

Jack extended an arm to Sarah, and she met his embrace. "We look forward to having you in our family. You are a special young lady, and we love you like a daughter already."

Sarah couldn't help but let a tear fall, as she recalled the first time that she met Mr. Patrick. "I love you too, Mr. Patrick."

He chuckled. "Do you think you could call me Jack?"

She smiled. "I would like that, Jack."

David cleared his throat. "Well, it's obvious who the *favorite* is around here."

They all laughed, and Liz put her hands on her hips. "I don't know whether to give you a hug and say 'congratulations' or knock you upside the head for scaring the life out of me."

David grabbed her. "I'd prefer the hug."

She wrapped her arms around his neck as he swung her around. "I love you, Dave. Congratulations. You couldn't have chosen any better than Sarah."

Sarah grinned. "That's *Miss Wonderful* to you."

Liz picked up one of the patio chair pillows and tossed it at her friend.

David laughed as he looked over at Sarah. "Welcome to the family."

That night, Sarah had dinner with her future in-laws, and everything was delicious. It seemed that Maria had pulled out all the stops for the celebratory meal. Filet mignon and shrimp, baked potatoes, Caesar salad, and chocolate cobbler for dessert. She had even placed a lovely red rose at Sarah's plate.

After the meal, they all made their way to the great room, and Elizabeth brought out her dad's guitar and handed it to Sarah.

"Play the one that you accompanied John on. You know, the one about hiding in the rock."

Sarah was a little surprised at Elizabeth's request, but she took the instrument and began to strum the chords. When she had finished, Mary asked that she play "It Is Well with My Soul," but Elizabeth stepped over to sit beside Sarah and draped an arm around her shoulders.

"Before you play the next song, I thought I would give you and Dave a wedding gift." She looked at David, who was sitting by Mary, next to the piano. "Come over here, Dave. I want to give it to both of you at the same time."

David got up and walked over to the hearth where Sarah was seated. "Oh, come on, Liz. We didn't expect you to get us a gift."

Liz gave him an amused grin. "I'm your sister. I'll give you a gift when I'm good and ready. Here." She handed him an envelope.

He turned it over in his hand a few times to examine it. "Well, I know it isn't a toaster."

Liz rolled her eyes and moved over to sit on the sofa. "For heaven sake, just open it."

David opened the note and Sarah leaned over to read with him.

It read,
Congratulations, Dave and Sarah!
Your sister in Christ,
Elizabeth.

David and Sarah looked at each other, back down at the card, and then at each other again. They both slowly looked over at Elizabeth, who was grinning ear-to-ear, as a tear made its way down her cheek.

Sarah ran over to wrap Elizabeth in a big hug while David could only sit and wipe tears.

Jack and Mary were looking confused. "Are you guys going to share this with your father and me, or do we have to guess?" Mary looked at Elizabeth. "You're not getting married, too, are you?"

David walked over to Mary and handed her the card. "Read it aloud, so Dad can hear."

Mary took the card and began to read. "Congratulations, Dave and Sarah! Your sister in Chr..." Mary's voice broke and she began to cry. "Your sis...ter...in Christ, Elizabeth."

Jack began to laugh and wipe tears at the same time. Sarah finally stopped hugging Elizabeth long enough to ask, "When did this happen?"

Elizabeth smiled. "The night that I talked to you. What you said made sense. After I got off the phone with you, I read about Jesus's crucifixion, and I also read the verses that Dave had jotted down for me. For the first time in my life, I saw who Jesus really is, and who *I* really am. I prayed that night and asked him to be my savior. I was dying to call and tell you, but I decided to wait until you both got back. Then, you really surprised me with your engagement announcement, so I decided to tell you tonight."

Jack stood and took a few weak steps over to Elizabeth. He took her hand on one side and Mary's on the other. David and Sarah joined in to make the circle complete. Jack bowed his head. "Dear, heavenly Father, I..." His voice trailed off, as the tears began to flow. He began again. "Dear heavenly Father, I thank you for making our family complete in you. We praise you and thank you for sending your Son to die on a cross for our sins, so that we can be together in heaven—a place where we'll never know pain or parting. Thank you for showing Elizabeth the truth of your Word. Help us to live each day with eternity in view. In Jesus's holy name I pray, amen."

Chapter Twenty-Nine

Monday morning, David rolled over and read the clock. Six thirty. He reached over to retrieve his cell from the nightstand. It was Steve. He gave a sleepy "Hello."

"Hey, man. I guess congratulations are in order."

David yawned as he rolled over on his back. "Thanks. Don't you ever sleep? I gave you the weekend off, and this is the thanks I get? A phone call at six thirty?"

Steve chuckled. "I have a special brew of coffee and hot chocolate twice a day."

David raked a hand through his hair. "That sounds too stout for me. Not to mention, dangerous. By the way, how did you know that congratulations were in order? I only told you that I was having dinner with Sarah."

He could hear Steve's grin across the connection. "Man, if I was that deaf and blind, you'd need to hire a new security man."

David gave an amused grunt. "That obvious, huh?"

"Yep, that obvious. Besides, Sarah's awesome. If I could find a girl that nice, I might consider giving up the single life. But I think you got the last one. Some guys have all the luck." Steve was silent for a moment and then turned serious. "Uh...I need to talk to you sometime today if you've got a few minutes."

"Sure. I'll be free around eleven. I was planning on coming home for an early lunch before I have to be back at the park this afternoon. We could talk then. Will that work?"

"Sounds good. Later."

"See ya."

David clicked off his phone and stepped out of the bed to stretch and head for a hot shower. Steve had sounded serious...too serious.

Steve walked into the kitchen and over to the breakfast nook to sit at the table across from David. Maria came over to set down a bowl of steaming, hot potato soup, a chicken salad croissant with fresh fruit, and coffee.

He removed his hat and bowed his head for a moment then scooped up a helping of soup before plopping his hat back on his head. "Thanks, Maria. This smells great."

Maria smiled and gave David a serious glance before leaving the kitchen. Steve looked across the table. "Everything alright?"

"I told her we needed to talk privately. Besides, I should be asking *you* that question. Is everything alright?"

Steve picked up a small spoon and began stirring his coffee. "Yeah." He stopped stirring and leaned back in his chair to give a long sigh. "Dave, you know I've been praying about going back to Texas. I got a call from Captain Sawyers last week, wanting me to consider coming back. They're overworked and understaffed. Then, my grandmother called to tell me that Grandpa's not well, and I feel guilty not being there for them." He leaned forward to cross his arms on the table and pushed up his cowboy hat with one finger. "Dave, I need to go back to Texas. I hate to throw it to you now, with you gettin' married and all, but I know what I've got to do."

David sighed. "I knew this day would eventually come, but I was hoping it would be later than sooner." He leaned back and looked across the table. "You're like the brother I never had. I'm going to miss having you here, but I understand your position. If I were in your shoes, I'd feel the same way. Family is everything, and I wouldn't want you to stay here when your family needs you there. When do you plan to leave?"

"I know you're gonna be busy gettin' ready for the wedding. Between gettin' married and baseball, you won't have much time to look for a replacement. And since I don't wanna leave you hangin', I'd like to find someone else before I go, if that's all right. I know of a man that, in my opinion, would be perfect for the job. I also know he'd be interested."

David leaned his arms on the table. "Steve, you know I trust your judgment completely, but I'd like to hear about him. What's his background?"

"He worked with me in the Texas Rangers Division for a few years before taking a job in Montana with the SBI. He's a few years younger than me, and he's a great Christian man. He told me about Jesus when I wasn't a believer yet, and he was one of the few people I knew at the time that actually lived it. He made an impression on me that stuck. If we ate lunch together, he always took off his hat and gave thanks for the food, and I never heard him curse, even in the tightest situations. As for his professional abilities, he's one of the best. I've tried to stay in contact with him over the years. I know he's gettin' burnt out with the SBI and would be interested in private security. I can set up a meeting with him if you think he's what you're looking for."

David shook his head. "If you think he's right for the job, that's good enough for me. Go ahead and contact him. If he's interested, hire him. What did you say his name was?"

Steve grinned. "Tony Bearclaw."

David's eyebrows rose. "Bearclaw. Native American?"

"Right down to his moccasins."

"You're kidding, right?"

Steve laughed. "I'm kidding. Tony is strictly a cowboy boot man. He's from the Blackfeet Tribe and grew up on the reservation in Montana. He's a gentleman all the way, but if there's trouble, you definitely want him on your side. If he'll take the job, I think I can get him here by the time you're back from the honeymoon."

"Sounds good to me."

The two men stood and shook on it. David held his hand firmly. "Thanks, Steve…for everything."

Steve gave a nod and walked out of the kitchen without a word.

Chapter Thirty

The wedding at The Valley Chapel was simple. Rebekah was the maid of honor with Elizabeth and Jennifer as bridesmaids. Mr. Patrick stood with David as best man, with John and Steve as groomsmen. Sarah was lovely in her white gown, carrying a bouquet of red roses, as she was escorted down the aisle by her father.

Pastor Mosbey asked, "Who gives this woman in holy matrimony?"

Mike Phillips spoke up. "Her mother and I." He leaned over to give Sarah a kiss on the cheek. "I love you."

She squeezed his arm. "I love you too. Thanks for being such an awesome dad."

He smiled down at her then placed her hand in David's before being seated. He took his place beside Katherine, who was already wiping tears. He leaned over to whisper in her ear. "Well, Katherine I knew we would lose her sooner or later, but I confess that I was hoping it would be later."

Katherine wiped another tear and gave him a wry grin. "And just think. We've got four more to go."

He chuckled. "No way. I've already decided that I'm going to lock Rebekah in her room till she's forty."

After the ceremony, David and Sarah stood outside the little church to receive well wishes from each guest, followed by numerous photographs. The early April weather was unseasonably cold, and Sarah was happy that she had decided on a long-sleeved gown. Rebekah had also made a long, white, satin cape with white fur trim for Sarah to wear over her wedding gown. As she stood in the chilly air to exchange handshakes and hugs with the guests, she was thankful for Rebekah's thoughtfulness in making the cape. She must have worked on it day and night to have gotten it completed in time for the wedding.

Robert Martin was the first one in line. "Congratulations, Dr. Philli…uh…I mean, Mrs. Patrick."

Sarah laughed. "It's okay, Mr. Martin. It'll take me a while to get used to the title too."

He nervously looked at the ground. "Martha and Elsie wanted me to send their regrets. Elsie wasn't feeling well, and Martha felt that she should stay home with her."

His face was flushed, as he was clearly embarrassed. He must have found out what his wife and niece had tried to do. Sarah placed a gentle hand on his arm. "I understand, Mr. Martin. Thank you for coming. And please give my regards to Elsie and Mrs. Martin as well. I hope Elsie is feeling better soon."

Robert stepped over to David and shook his hand as he looked with deep sincerity. "Congratulations, David. You're a blessed man."

"Yes, sir."

David had overheard Sarah's conversation, and as Mr. Martin walked away, he leaned over to whisper, "You're amazing."

Sarah looked at him and lowered her voice. "I like Mr. Martin, he's a nice man. I feel a bit sorry for him, though. He seemed so embarrassed, but he couldn't help what happened."

Steve walked up to give Sarah a hug, and David slapped him on the back. "All right, all right! That's enough."

Steve and Sarah started laughing, and David shook his hand. "It's not going to be the same around here without you."

Steve winked at Sarah. "You don't need me anymore. You've got Sarah to keep you in line now."

Sarah put a hand on his arm. "I hope you'll come and visit as often as you can, Steve. I'm going to miss you. Oh, and don't forget to visit my grandparents. I told them you would come, and they'll be expecting you."

Steve tipped his big cowboy hat. "I'll be sure and do that, ma'am. And if you're ever down Texas way, be sure to look me up."

David gave his friend a hearty hug. "Thanks for everything, buddy."

Steve gave him a wide grin. "That was a nice hug, Dave, but I'd rather hug the bride."

David laughed and gave him a slap on the back. "Get outta here."

Liz came to hug her new sister-in-law good-bye. "You two have a safe trip."

Sarah smiled. "We will. But I have no idea where I'm going. Since David has to be back in three days, he has insisted that it be a surprise." Sarah gave her one more hug. "Thanks for being a great friend. I'm glad you're my sister-in-law, but I'm even more thankful that you're my sister in Christ."

When Elizabeth faced her, there were tears in her eyes. "I'm glad too."

She stepped over to hug her big brother. "I'm so happy for you, Dave. Congratulations."

Elizabeth wiped a tear and chuckled. "See, I was right. I knew you liked her."

David twitched her nose. "Wrong again. I loved her. Thanks, Liz. I love you. You're the best." He lowered his voice as he whispered in her ear. "And God loves you too."

"Yeah. I'm glad that I know that, now." She wiped another tear and moved on through the line.

Sarah gave Jennifer a hug, while David gripped John's hand in a firm handshake.

"You're still bringing the children to the baseball game Friday night, aren't you?"

John slapped him on the shoulder. "You bet. We wouldn't miss it."

Jennifer was excited. "Having a belated wedding reception after the game and watching fireworks was a great idea! The kids will love it!"

Sarah glanced at David. "I can't take all the credit. It was a David's idea. We wanted to do something for our family and friends, and that particular suite is special to us. It's where David proposed."

Jennifer's eyebrows scrunched together as she let out an "Ooooh! How sweet!"

John took her arm and gave David a wry grin. "Thanks a lot. Now that she knows how romantic a guy can be, I'll have to come up with something good for our anniversary next month."

As the last photo was taken, the limousine pulled up. David was helping Sarah to the car when he quietly whispered in her ear. "Look, snow."

She turned her back to toss the little bouquet of flowers directly toward her sister. Rebekah reached for the bouquet, and as she caught it, she immediately froze in amazement. With her face to the sky, she stood in wonder at the beautiful flakes falling lazily to the ground. When she looked back at Sarah, she was smiling. Sarah blew her a kiss and mouthed, "Good-bye, Becksy. I love you." A tear made its way down Rebekah's cheek as she blew her sister a kiss good-bye and began waving.

David stepped inside the limo and wrapped his arms around Sarah. They waved good-bye and began their life's journey together. David lifted her hand and brushed a kiss across her ring finger. He looked down at the little cluster of diamonds with the sparkling ruby in the center and gazed into Sarah's eyes. "Who can find a virtuous woman? For her price is far above rubies."

Dear Reader,

I hope you have enjoyed David and Sarah's love story as much as I enjoyed writing it. It is my prayer that you also know the most ultimate love of all…God's love. He loved us so much that he gave his son, Jesus Christ, to die on a cross and pay our sin debt. Salvation is available to all who will believe. Have you received this free gift of salvation? If not, you can receive the Lord Jesus Christ right now.

A) **A**cknowledge that you are a sinner in need of a Savior: "For all have sinned and come short of the glory of God" (Romans 3:23). "He that believeth on Him is not condemned: but he that believeth not is condemned already, because he hath not believed in the name of the only begotten Son of God" (John 3:18).

B) **B**elieve on the Lord Jesus Christ and His sacrifice on the cross of Calvary as a payment for your sin. "For God so loved the world, that He gave His only Son, that whosoever believeth in Him should not perish, but have everlasting life" (John 3:16).

C) **C**onfess your sin and ask Jesus to forgive you and be Lord of your life. "If we confess our sins, He is faithful and just to forgive us our sins, and to cleanse us from all unrighteousness" (1 John 1:9).

I love to hear from my readers! You may contact me at:
www.moorehousemedia.org

Made in the USA
Columbia, SC
20 October 2024